Praise for Stephen May

'Stephen May manages to balance hilarity and sadness in nearly every sentence.'

Suzanne Berne, author of Orange Prize winner
A Crime in the Neighbourhood

'Stephen May has the sharp eye of David Nicholls and the verve of Kate Atkinson.'

Suzannah Dunn, author of
The Confession of Katherine Howard

Stronger than Skin

'Gripping from the first page, this addictive tale of toxic love gone wrong will have you cancelling your plans for the rest of the week.' *Sunday Mirror*

'Another great insight into the male psyche. I read this in a day.' Jane Harris, author of *Sugar Money*

Wake Up Happy Every Day

'A compelling read' *The Guardian*

'Acerbic and funny' *New York Times*

Life! Death! Prizes!

'A warm novel, written with a wry wit.'
Kate Saunders, *The Times*

'Raw, funny, heartfelt . . . full of surprising tenderness and hope.' Kennedy

Stephen May is the author of five novels including *Life! Death! Prizes!* which was shortlisted for the Costa Novel Award and The Guardian Not The Booker Prize. He has also been shortlisted for the Wales Book of the Year and is a winner of the Media Wales Reader's Prize. He has also written plays, as well as for television and film. He lives in West Yorkshire.

By the same author

TAG
Life! Death! Prizes!
Wake Up Happy Every Day
Stronger than Skin

STEPHEN MAY

WE DON'T DIE OF DIE OF LOVE

SANDSTONE PRESS

First published in Great Britain by
Sandstone Press Ltd
Willow House
Stoneyfield Business Park
Inverness
IV2 7PA
Scotland

www.sandstonepress.com

The publisher acknowledges subsidy from Creative
Scotland towards publication of this volume.

ISBN: 978-1-912240-74-6
ISBNe: 978-1-912240-75-3

Cover design by Stuart Brill
Typeset by Biblichor Ltd, Edinburgh
Printed and bound by CPI Group (UK) Ltd, Croydon, CR0 4YY

To Caron

1

THE BREAKFAST RUSH

Here I am inching out of bed at 5am, careful not to disturb my sleeping wife. Selena can be fierce if woken suddenly. Here I am standing at the marble worktop while the dry heaviness of sleep lifts, while another dawn gathers itself outside the window. Here I am using the vintage coffee grinder she bought for me. This is soothing exercise first thing in the morning. Almost meditative. Quality beans rattling into the business end. Spicy Java, way better than the ones we use in Ernies.

Here I am passing the time as that good coffee chuckles on the hob, trying to do something useful. Putting away the stuff in the dishwasher. In a few minutes it'll be late enough to risk the radio, to listen to the usual voices do their practised routine. Older man grumbling against the dying of the light. Severely flirty younger woman almost audibly eye-rolling next to him.

Somebody murdered. Some war somewhere. Time for the sport. Time for the weather.

Always different, always the same. The repetition embedded in the format always comforting even when the content is scary. This is how radio works. Reassures even as it alarms. The world will be a more frightening place when it dies, when it finally goes the way of print.

For the entire time Selena and I have been together – the whole thirty-one years – this is how I've got us moving into the long corridor of the day. For the first two decades the fuel injection of choice was tea, but at some point in the early twenty-first century it became coffee: two barista-style Americanos made in a proper stove-top pot. Hers white with one xylitol, mine black and unsweetened.

By six I'm back up the stairs where Selena, more or less awake now, gives me a low-voltage smile – that mouth, those lips, those teeth, the laughing beads of her eyes – and my heart twitches.

I give her a quick digest of the lead stories on the *Today* programme, and in return she gives me a brief run-through of the day's movements and appointments. The things I need to remember. The things I should pick up from town when I have a minute, after the breakfast rush has faded and before the lunch rush starts. This is a joke, sort of. These so-called rushes are of the most sluggish kind. I try not to rise to it. *Yeah, yeah. Don't worry. I'm across it.* Or words to that effect.

This is how it is. Every day the same. Always.

So you'd think I'd know enough to be alarmed when, the day after my fifty-eighth birthday, I woke from restless dreams to find my wife coming into the bedroom with weak Nescafé in my best mug, the vintage Batman mug, the one I hardly use myself for fear it will fade in the dishwasher. Idiot that I am, blind fool that I am, I didn't even give it a second's thought. I just accepted the drink and said thank you. Thank you.

People have said – at least Selena has said, our children have said – that I can be a bit thick when it comes to picking up signals about how people are feeling. I am, apparently, tone-deaf to the music made by the body, to

2

the songs that sail beneath the spoken word, but – honestly – looking back, I'm sure that on this particular day there were no signals to pick up. Maybe she was frowning a bit and that wasn't like her. No hints otherwise of what was to come.

After she handed me the mug, Selena studied me for a long moment.

'What?' I said. 'What?'

Selena took a breath and came right out with it. Her voice quiet, dry, carefully neutral. 'We are not happy, Luke. At least, we're not happy enough.'

Then it was tumbling out. All the words in a rush like sparkling water over ice, all cracking and fizz.

'We both know it . . . Neither of us are getting any younger . . . So we should, yeah, we should split up . . . Give ourselves a chance of living a different kind of life before it is too late . . .'

And so on. Her whole speech was two minutes maybe. Tops.

'What do you think?' She was biting her lip, there was a flush high on her cheekbones.

What did I think? I know what I *did*. I laughed. Actually laughed. A nervous response, I swear. I wasn't really able to think anything. Anyway, my laughing pissed her off.

'I'm serious,' she said.

She was. I could see the little tells, the things I should have spotted earlier. The tension in her neck, the hard compression of her lips. The way she was dressed. Not how she was dressed, but the simple fact of her being dressed at all. On a normal day, Selena took an age to get ready but today she was all prepped for action in jeans and a grey hoodie. Pragmatic and inconspicuous clothing, she could be going on to take part in a bank robbery.

She must have got her clothes on while I was sleeping, which meant she had got things ready the night before.

3

Stashed in the bathroom maybe, so she could rise early and put them on without disturbing me. An assassin's thinking: do the job, get out unnoticed. Perhaps she was up here sorting out her outfit while I was downstairs reading birthday cards and standing them up on the mantelpiece.

She told me now she was sorry. Over and over. Sorry, sorry, sorry. Yeah, yeah. We sat in silence. Me in bed, her on the chair by the dressing table. The dressing table itself, chosen together in an auction room in 1993 or 1994 was, I saw now, clear of many of its usual bottles and tubes, its small pots of lotion. Its brushes and its pencils. Clear space where there was usually clutter. The air growing dense and squeezed, as if the walls were moving closer.

I asked her how long she'd felt like this.

'It's been building for a while now. I've been trying to keep things together, trying to make it work but . . .' She shrugged, suddenly helpless. But. But.

I closed my eyes. Somewhere in the distance there was a siren. Someone's week getting off to a bad start. Maybe a worse start than mine. No comfort in that. Closer to home were pigeons and their self-satisfied cooing. The rumble of traffic, a dog barking. The radio playing to no one in the kitchen. News of an earthquake somewhere. The newsreader's voice both serious and also somehow suggesting that it was okay, there were not many dead and none of them British.

Selena asked if I was going to speak at all, ever. 'I didn't realise it wasn't working,' I said.

She shrugged again. That, this shrug said, was the whole problem right there. The whole story of her and me.

'You've never said anything,' I said.

She sighed, rolled her eyes. 'I've been trying to. Anyway. You think we're okay? You think we're still

4

good together? Don't tell me you haven't thought about splitting up.'

'I haven't thought about splitting up,' I said. And it was true, I hadn't, not once. In thirty-one years it hadn't crossed my mind. Not seriously.

'Crap,' she said.

That was it. All it took. We were off. At each other's throats.

You said—

Yeah, but you said—

You did—

Yeah, but you did and anyway that was because—

Well, what about when—

I stopped it all before we really got going. Held up a hand. Went to the bathroom. Closed the door. Locked it. First time I'd done that in years.

I looked at myself in the mirror. Did I look worse or better than a fifty-eight-year-old should? I didn't know. Couldn't tell. I did know there was twisting in my guts. I felt sick. I counted to ten. Slowly. Forced myself to breathe.

I needed to get shaved, to get myself together for work and, besides, I'd just got the idea that hot and total war was what she wanted. That she'd be relieved if I got mad, if I said hurtful, unforgiveable things. That she maybe wanted me to spit out the unsayable, the unthinkable. The things you can't come back from. Maybe she wanted me to break my favourite mug by chucking it against the wall. Coffee all over the designer wallpaper that cost us an arm and a leg. Perhaps she felt that my anger would make it easier for her. Put her in the right somehow. So, better to do the opposite. I would be reasonable instead. Competitively reasonable. The most reasonable anyone has ever been about anything. Infuriatingly reasonable. Unreasonably reasonable.

5

I opened the bathroom door. Selena was just outside. Arms folded, lips pursed. Face flushed. Eyes blazing. So tense it looked like the bones of her face were straining against the skin. Beautiful. She looked beautiful.

'I've got to get ready,' I said.

Our faces were about an inch apart. I wondered what she'd do if I kissed her now.

'You don't think this is worth talking about,' she said. It was a statement not a question, and unfair because I know she didn't want to talk either, she just wanted me to want to.

'Work. I've got work.'

'Yeah,' she said. 'The "breakfast rush".' She did the quote thing in the air with her fingers. God, I hate it when people do that. Had Selena ever done it before? I didn't think so.

'You don't think Zoe and Wes can cope?' she said.

'I don't want them to have to cope.'

She sighed and turned away.

From back inside the bathroom, I heard her go downstairs, taking them two at a time like she always did.

2

YOGHURT WITH STRAWBERRIES

I didn't hear the front door open and close but by the time I was downstairs, Selena had definitely gone. The radio was off. There was a letter on the kitchen table. An A4 page taken from the printer, her writing a scrawl, large but still hard to read. She had written fast with the clear intention of getting it finished and getting out of the house before I came down to the kitchen.

Dear Luke, I'm sorry . . . That word again. Sometimes it seems sorry is the easiest word. But this apology was for the way she had told me, not for what she'd said. *It didn't come out how I wanted. The timing was all wrong. I should have waited until the evening, when we could have talked properly. With wine maybe* . . .

With wine. Like we would if we were discussing where to go on holiday next.

She wrote that, seeing me lying there, oblivious to what was going on in her head, well, she knew she couldn't spend another day with this on her conscience, so she had rushed it, just blurted it out and that maybe that hadn't been the best thing. But at least it was done now. Now we could get on with thinking about practicalities. She wrote that she knew that we would still be friends again when the dust had settled, that we shared too much to lose that. She still respected me. She still loved me. Probably as much as she ever had. She just didn't want to be married to me.

I scrunched that vindication up and shoved it deep into the food-waste bin, got it right down among the coffee grounds, the banana peel and the onion skins.

Practicalities.

What did I do then? I washed my hands. Rinsed off the food bin cack and then did what I do every morning: lined up my phone, my keys, my glasses and my wallet on the kitchen table. I do this little roll call to make sure the essentials of life are present and correct before placing them in my briefcase. My briefcase was a vintage tan leather one, like something an Oxbridge lecturer might use rather than a cook. It was, like nearly everything half decent I owned, a present from Selena. Something she'd sourced for my fifty-third. Maybe fifty-second. Sometime around then.

I headed out to the car. The gravel snapped, crackled and popped under my shoes. There had been a light frost, cold for early September. I could see my breath in the stinging air. There were still bees and butterflies but there wouldn't be for long. I zapped the Audi open. There was the comforting bloop, the soothing blink.

Sitting behind the wheel I felt reassured somehow. Hard to feel that the world is going completely to shit when you are cocooned by old but high-quality *Vorsprung durch Technik*, then, as I came out of the drive, I very nearly flattened a cyclist. My fault. I didn't see her despite the fact she was wearing a Puffa jacket in vivid yellow.

The gesture she made was crude but justified. I had no excuse. I didn't see her because I wasn't looking.

I thought again about the evening before. A fish-pie from the freezer with a glass of white wine. Yoghurt with strawberries for dessert. The half-watching of some

Netflix thing, the half-reading of articles embedded in links sent to us by friends, the half-listening to a couple of albums – Bowie's *Low*, Kate Bush's live album. Then, in bed, a few pages of books. Selena: Kate Atkinson. Me: Steig Larsson. The whole evening couldn't have been more ordinary. A birthday in the lowest possible key. I had assumed we'd celebrate properly at the weekend.

I cast my mind back further: what about over the last weeks? Any warnings there? Nothing. We'd even had sex not long back.

Suddenly I regretted keeping my temper earlier, regretted just getting ready for work because, well, because, fuck work. I had a lot to say now. I should have thrown that mug against the wall. I should have watched that unforgivably under-powered Nescafé splatter across that overpriced wallpaper.

I drove towards work for a while but it was no good. My neck hurt, my eyes were sore. There was a taste in my mouth, metallic and sour. I pulled into a side street, turned the engine off and called her. The voicemail kicked in. I didn't leave a message and was about to pull away from the kerb when my phone pinged.

You okay? A text from Selena. No kiss, I noticed. The first time ever she'd texted without a kiss? Maybe.

I called again. Voicemail again. I was being screened out. Text was clearly how we were going to do this. How very fucking modern.

There was rage building again and I welcomed it in, the heat and pressure of it. The energy of it. The way it hurt.

I pecked out: *What about the kids?*

Feeble. Wished I could call it back.

No reply for ages. A minute at least. Then: *Kids will be fine. They're grown-ups now. More or less. They'll have two places to come back to instead of one.*

A few seconds passed, while I tried and failed to think of a reply but then another ping. She had more to say. *I know it's a shock. I know it must be confusing. I've had a lot more time to get used to it. But it's for the best, I really believe that. For both of us. And the hard part is done now.*

I was thinking: is it? Is it really? Will the kids be fine? Really? Yes, so they're twenty-three and nineteen. But kids stay toddlers where their parents are concerned. Our kids – whatever they say, however they act, however old they are – always want a cuddle or a treat. Always want their parents to be waiting exactly where they left them in case they need them. They don't want two homes to come back to, their certainties blown apart when their backs are turned.

I wasn't getting into all that. Not by text.

I jabbed out something else: *We had sex last week.*

Another long half-minute before she replied. *Three weeks ago. And it's what helped me decide.*

I called again. I wasn't letting that go. We were good at sex. Inventive. Abandoned. Sex is something we've always had even when we've been getting on each other's nerves.

Voicemail again. I smacked the steering wheel with my palms. Yelled as loud as I could. Couldn't help myself. Wordless howling. Didn't feel better afterwards exactly, but de-pressurised maybe. Not quite as likely to burst.

I looked around at the neighbourhood I was in. Executive housing. Two-car garages. I didn't want any curtain-twitching working-from-home middle manager phoning the plods.

I typed: *??????*

The response was almost instant. *Come on. It's become a bit of a duty. Last thing to be ticked off the to-do list. We've been going through the motions. You must feel that too. Before last time it had been months.*

I called again. Voicemail again. No choice but to keep texting. Caps lock.

ANSWER YOUR PHONE.

The reply was quick at least: *I don't want to get into a shouting match. I want to keep it civilised.*

A thirty-one-year partnership dissolved by text. Was that civilised or the sign of a civilisation in its death throes?

I took a breath. I took caps lock off. Didn't want to be loud, too shouty. Wanted to express exactly how I was feeling, needed to call on my old journalistic skills to put down exactly the right words in exactly the right order.

Fuck you, Selena.

Again, the almost instant reply. *We'll talk later. When you're calm. Xx*

Kisses now. Kisses *now*. They stung. I was thinking, if she uses emojis, I will really lose it. She's a fan of the emoji, is my wife. Has totally embraced them. I struggle a bit myself. I hadn't ever thought of myself as on the spectrum before the emoji era but these days I often get texts and have no idea what people are trying to say to me. I can work out happy, sad and that crying with laughter face. Anything else I'm never 100 per cent about. Part of the whole bit-thick-about-picking-up-signals thing, no doubt.

I sat back in the seat. I closed my eyes. It took a while but I thought of something else to say.

Why now? Why today? Why not last year or last week? Why not yesterday? I was angry, yes, but I was also genuinely curious – what prompts someone to finally chuck the hand grenade into a relationship? Why choose one moment rather than another?

We couldn't split up yesterday. Not on your birthday.

The phone went. I answered it already shouting and without checking the screen.

'Couldn't do it on my birthday? This is bullshit! This is—'

'Luke?'

Wasn't Selena. Was work. 'Oh, Zoe, sorry.'

'You all right?'

'Yeah, it's just—'

'Good. Are you on your way? Because we're a bit under the cosh here.'

I thought about reminding her about which one of us owned the place and which one waited tables for just over minimum wage. But really, what would have been the point? Not one for hierarchies, is Zoe. Not one to obey the normal courtesies of line management. It was one of the things I liked about her.

The fight left me. I felt it go and a hollow space open up where it used to be.

'Yeah, sorry. On my way. I'll be there in two ticks.'

3

SOMETHING WEIRD

Earnshaws – Ernies, if you're a local – sits on a corner plot in the bruised and battered part of the city. Stonebeck. Motorway on one side, canal on the other and 500 acres of tightly meshed terraced housing, empty warehouses and derelict workshops in between.

You know what Selena used to say about Stonebeck? She said that if it was a person it would be a small-time crook. A bloke with anger management issues. Someone who doesn't know how to look after himself. Someone who wakes up with a headache every day. Someone who goes out to the shops in the afternoon and comes back home at midnight without his shoes. He'd be malnourished too. There are more fast-food places per head of population here there than anywhere else in England. It's the home of shops called Boozebuster and Vapes-R-Us. Multiple places to get your scratch cards and your cider but nowhere to get a lettuce.

So, yes, it's a hard place to love but those of us that do love it, we love it fiercely, unconditionally.

The place is changing a bit though. I've noticed a trickle of the bravest of the middle-class young professionals moving in recently. Very contemporary types. Men with moisturised cheeks above well-managed beards. Women in donkey jackets riding bikes. The occasional same-sex couple holding hands. A yoga studio replacing one of the eFag emporiums. Enough early signs of gentrification so that you can imagine that one day the area will be very different. It'll be renamed Southside or Southbank or something, redesignated an Urban Village, our equivalent of Manchester's famous Northern Quarter. The next 'Shoreditch of the North' even. A place the Sunday papers will start writing about in those Let's All Move To . . . columns produced in their sleep by journos with no intention of ever moving out of London.

Already I'd had to start ordering in the almond milk, had to keep a dozen varieties of herbal teas alongside the Yorkshire Breakfast. Jasmine with lemon. Cardamom and Ginger.

I've had Ernies fifteen years, ever since journalism spat me out. Took it over when it was an old-school working man's greasy spoon. Tried to keep what was good about it. Proper portion sizes, freshly cooked at decent prices. Our eggs free-range, our bacon sourced from the happiest pigs. Our tea always strong. Our coffee good – though not as good as the stuff I have at home.

Also, we don't object to babies or dogs. Not even the Staffies that seem to stare at our human customers with fentanyl eyes. Not even the toddlers with their cheerful profanities and their nose rings.

When I got there the place was nearly empty. One big bloke in a neon lime hi-vis vest was wiping egg yolk and tomato juice from his plate with a slice of fried bread. Zoe twitchily impatient by his table, waiting to clear his plate away. She looked around as I came in.

'Under the cosh?' I said.

'Should have been here earlier,' she said. 'Ram-packed we were.'

Zoe was twenty-nine but looked younger. Turquoise hair, a dozen piercings in her ears and others in her nose and her lips. Tattoos on her arms, shoulders and neck. Abstract, vaguely Maori-ish swirls and blocks all in thick black, standing out bold against her pale skin. She also had a PhD in history awarded for a thesis about the development of European legal systems in the late medieval period. She could have been teaching at a university somewhere but Dr Zoe Vargo preferred it down among the hard hats, down among those who cleaned their plates with their fried slice. She's also Hungarian, not that you'd have known from her English which was impeccably West Yorkshire.

I headed through to the kitchen to say hi to Wes. The kitchen was spotless as usual and smelled of lemon and vinegar. Wes ran a tight ship. No matter how early I was in he was in before me. He's a grafter.

'Sorry I missed the breakfast shift, Wes. Got a bit held up.'

I wondered what I'd say if he wanted a fuller explanation, but I thought he wouldn't push it. He never did. He never asked anything even remotely personal. Wes learned his cookery skills at her majesty's pleasure which is where I guess he also learned to cultivate a lack of curiosity. At six foot three and big with it, Wes could project a sense of quiet menace, even when he was just poaching an egg or buttering a teacake. Wes was good at being left alone. Carried with him a highly effective intimacy repellent. Very useful on those occasions when we had trouble-making fuckwits in. A silent, frowning Wes, arms folded, just beaming out his calm and steady look – a patient spider at the centre of his web – was enough to get even the most pointlessly belligerent to pay up and clear off.

'It's okay,' he said now. 'Breakfast rush wasn't too bad.'

I asked him about his weekend. Also okay and not too bad, apparently.

He didn't ask about mine.

* * *

The craze for brunch as the major meal of the day had not reached us yet. Post-breakfast is still a dead zone. Wes made up some sandwich orders, I did some paperwork out at my favourite corner table and Zoe pissed about on social media. There was a lot of exasperated sighing and theatrical eye-rolling at what she read. I'd learned to ignore all that.

After a while she said, 'It seems the three main people that want to fuck me are a married man, an engaged man and a man who lives with his girlfriend. What is wrong with me?'

'The three main people?' I said.

'Yeah,' she said. 'I'm in a bit of a drought.'

I couldn't tell whether she was serious. It's often hard to tell with Zoe.

Then Wes had a break and Zoe took over making up the sandwich orders. During his break Wes did something weird. He read a book. Specifically, he opened up a hardback copy of Jane Eyre. Reader, I freaked out at this. Usually, whenever Wes had a break we spent it wittering about football. I don't really care much about the old beautiful game – twenty-two millionaire mummy's boys kicking a bladder around, who gives a shit, etc. – but today I found I was looking forward to it.

I did a pantomime shocked face as Wes settled into an ostentatious Man-at-Work pose. His back turned towards me, his shoulders hunched, the force-field in full operation. I knew he could see me watching him from the corner of his eye, but he ignored me. The silence did my brain in after a while. And by 'after a while' I mean 'after about thirty-eight seconds'.

'Got a new girlfriend, Wes?' I said. 'Posh, is she?'

'Don't be an arse, Luke,' he said. 'I've joined a book club, that's all. No biggie.'

'I didn't even know men were allowed to join book clubs.'

I let it go after that. Didn't like how I sounded, to be honest. Tone was wrong. We often took the mick out of each other at work of course. You had to be on your mettle at Ernies. Had to bring your A-game banter. Had to be able to keep your end up, not just with your co-workers (Zoe could do bantz in five languages) but with the customers too. They're quick and they're sharp in Stonebeck. But I had heard a grating note under my words. Some needle there.

Zoe came back out and grimaced at her phone for a while.

'Hey, listen to this,' she said. There was an icy edge to her voice.

I'm sure I heard a controlled, almost inaudible, but definitely present sigh of relief escape from Wes. I'm sure I saw his shoulders relax as he laid his book down on the table in front of him, as if given permission to put down some heavyish load. When she was sure she had our attention, Zoe read to us from her Samsung.

There's a reviews site that's used a lot in the trad-caff world – ChipAdvisor (see what they did there?) – and there were new posts about us. Not raves either. Three two-line reviews where Ernies got properly slagged for pretty much everything. We were rude, apparently, so insolent we could almost be French. We were lazy, forgetful, sloppy, perhaps on drugs. Our eggs were too hard or they were too runny. Our bacon was maggoty. Someone was convinced they'd seen mouse droppings in the bog. Someone else claimed we didn't recycle properly, swore they'd seen cardboard and plastic promiscuously entangled. These days there is no bigger crime than that.

Three one-star reviews. Bastards.

I've always tried not to let things like this hurt me too much, tried to remember that the general public don't know very much about anything. That's a thing that running a business tells you: the punters are lunatics. Especially the ones who take time out of a busy work schedule to write reviews on the interweb. There are people out there who write essay-length reviews of things like firelighters and screenwash.

What can you say? People are mad as arseholes. That's what you can say.

Wes headed back to the kitchen to peel and chop, to slice and dice. I wiped the tables again. That's the kind of boss I am. Leading by example. Unafraid to roll up my sleeves. Zoe wouldn't let me have it any other way.

Every now and then some random wandered in for a brew. Occasionally they'd have a pasty or a sausage roll then they wandered out again.

Radio 2 did its thing. That old music. Those irrepressible voices talking cheery rubbish. The traffic. A quiz.

Time passed.

About noon one of our first regulars appeared: Ken. A man of indeterminate age, dapper in sports jacket, jaunty tie and slacks. He led a practised routine. We all knew our parts. First he asked for something arcane, then he feigned outrage when we told him that it wasn't on the menu.

'What?' he said. 'What? Really? No sautéed kale? No pepper stuffed with calf's liver in a walnut jus? No truffle oil? But, Luke, these are basics. The very stuff of life. These are the bare necessities.' Which was the cue for him to croak out the song of that name. We waited patiently while he exhorted us to forget about our worries and our cares.

'What have you got?' he said, when he finally wheezed to a stop. 'What are the specials? What can you tempt me with?'

'There's shepherd's pie today,' said Zoe in her deadpan way.

'Ah, you know what, my lovely? I don't fancy your shepherd's today. I'll have a nice round of hot buttered toast. Do you think you can manage that, Wesley, my friend? A round of hot buttered toast?'

'I can try,' said Wes.

Ken never had shepherd's pie. He never had any of the specials. He only ever had hot buttered toast which he always complained about afterwards – not hot enough, not brown enough, not buttery enough – and which we always let him off paying for. See? People, the general public. Lunatics.

Ken was by no means the weirdest of the regulars. I found myself wondering if he'd been one of those to one-star us on Chip, but surely not. Surely free toast every day bought a little bit of loyalty?

Ken was the only customer until lunchtime proper when we got a bumper crop of Polish hard hats. A pageant of them queuing for teacakes, resplendent in hi-vis. There was some kind of flood alleviation work going on, so lots of demand for bacon. Some things in this life are very predictable and it's an Iron Law that hard hats – of whatever nationality – will always want hot processed pig.

Modern Britain is sustained by bacon baps.

When the lunch customers had gone, when I was back installed in Paperwork Corner juggling invoices – they never stop – Zoe plonked herself down opposite me. She offered to do the accounts, reminded me that I'm shit at it. I told her it was all right, that I needed the distraction. She gave me a long level look. It was unnerving.

'Right. Out with it,' she said.

'Out with what?'

'Out with whatever is making you so bloody pensive. It can't just be a few idiots writing crap about us. We've had worse.'

19

'Have we?'

'For sure. What about the guy that said he'd had the most dismal breakfast, complete with the most wrist-slittingly charmless service in a building that had all the congeniality of a 1980s job centre? What about that one?'

Some memory for quotes, that girl. Must have helped in the old thesis writing.

'It's not the reviews. Anyway, I'm fine.'

'Bollocks,' she said. She ran a hand through sea-coloured hair. Blew heavily in exasperation. 'Something's up.' She tallied up the evidence. Counted it off on her fingers, bullet pointed for me. One: I normally keep up a steady stream of grouchy observations throughout the day. I moan about young people, about old people, about people in general actually. Two: I argue with the radio news. Three: I ask her intrusive questions about her love life and then don't listen to the answers. Four: I hassle her about not wasting time in a café working for me but to get a decent job instead. Something with a future.

'There's been none of any of this today. You hardly reacted at all when I told you about all the dudes currently pursuing me. It's not like you. Ergo something's amiss. It's a bit worrying.'

'Am I really like that?'

'Yep, you are actually. The whole pensive thing was like, a relief at first, but now it's actually scaring me.'

Ah, sod it.

After I told her about Selena she was quiet, thoughtful, and I did feel better. A bit.

I asked her what she reckoned.

'You don't need to know my opinion.'

I insisted on it. This was a mistake.

'Sixty-year-old bloke splits up with his wife. I'm sorry, Luke, but there's nothing to get upset about here. Not really. You and Selena had a good marriage, a long

20

marriage and now it's come to an end. Turned out to have a sell-by date. Which is sad, but not that sad. Not when compared to, you know, wars in the Middle East or famine or child abuse or Ebola or, I don't know, motor neurone disease or any of the real suffering and pain that goes on everywhere every day.'

She told me that we don't die of love. Her point being that it was actually, you know, kind of indulgent to fall apart over something like this.

When she was finished, I wanted to fire her. Instead I just stood up, took my apron off and left it on the chair. I didn't look at her. Instead I looked at the motley collection of utility chairs and mix-and-match tables carefully stripped and sanded – mostly by Selena – and I was suddenly sick of the place.

'You and Wes can clear up here and lock up, can't you?'

'Luke,' she began. 'I just . . .'

But I had already turned my back, was already walking towards the front door. At the door I had to pause and grope around for the handle. My eyes were full of tears. I heard Zoe say my name again, but I didn't look round.

All the way home I wound myself up with what I should have said to Zoe. Because I know of course a marriage break-up isn't the same as a war or motor neurone disease, but we don't operate league tables of sorrow, do we? Normal people don't have a mental exchange rate that goes my case of shingles equals your dead pet rabbit. Or a tragic earthquake in Tibet equals, I don't know, 1,128 holiday cancellations, the closing of a car factory and the emphysema of Mrs Wood at number 58. Bad stuff is just bad stuff. Pain is just pain and whatever the presumed cause it grows until it fills up all the available space. You can't allot someone's suffering a precise value and grade it like it was a gold ring. This is 9-carat misery while that over there is where we keep the 18-carat stuff.

Just as no child has ever eaten their unwanted greens just because they were told that people in Africa are starving, so no one is helped by knowing how much worse off other people are. What you do on hearing people's tragedies – however small – is you put an arm around their shoulders and ask how you can help. You don't tell them that what they're feeling is a bit dumb.

Plus I'm not sixty. Not for ages.

Zoe knew all this though. She called four times before I got home. To apologise, I guess, though I didn't find out for sure because I didn't pick up and she didn't leave a message.

4

HANG IN THERE, MATE

First thing I did when I got in was call the kids.

Charlie didn't answer. His voicemail consisted of him slurring *do the thing*. I didn't do the thing. I tried to do the thing but somehow I couldn't find the words. *Hi, son, your mum has just left me. Can you give me a call?* just didn't sound right somehow. I re-recorded my message five times before giving up completely.

Moments later I called Grace and it was clear she didn't know what had happened with Selena. I asked her what she was up to and she chirruped merrily about auditions for the drama club, about how nice everyone was, so friendly but also so southern, so posh, with so many good clothes. She told me how they've all got cars. It's Fiat 500 Central these days in Sussex apparently, though there are also students with Teslas. Imagine that. She told me how everyone in her flat was off to Nando's tonight, but she was staying in because she wanted to get on with her reading.

'Can you believe that, Dad? I'm choosing Emily Brontë over a cheeky Nando's.'

'What is it with the Brontës and their unlikely modern readership?'

'Sorry?'

'Nothing. Just those girls seem to be having a bit of a

moment. Anyway, I'm shocked and stunned and very proud. Have you spoken to your mum recently?'

'A couple of days ago. Why?'

'No reason. But you should call her.' Then I gave her a standard dad pep talk. Couldn't help myself. The sort of speech that most fathers can reel off to their daughters without even thinking. I droned on about making sure she begins assignments as soon as they're set, about not letting her social life overwhelm her studies, about managing her money, about eating properly, about not walking around Brighton on her own drunk late at night, about not getting into the cars of strangers.

She laughed and reminded me that she was nineteen for God's sake and that I should have a little faith and did I go on at Charlie like this when he went to uni? She's right, I thought, I should have faith. She's a good kid. And no, I didn't nag at Charlie in the same way, but nevertheless, despite her rightness, I went on at her a bit more. Like I say, couldn't help myself. I reminded her that it is okay to say no to men who are pressurising her and that if she does fancy saying yes at all ever – and it's almost never a good idea – then she should take proper precautions. I was all like 'and I mean belt and braces, my girl'. God, it must have been exasperating to listen to. I annoyed myself. In the end Grace almost snapped at me, bit my head off.

'Okay, Dad, I'm hanging up now.'

I tried to row back. Told her I knew I'd gone over the top a bit. 'It's just that I worry. Your mum and me, we both worry.'

She laughed, mollified. She never stayed cross about anything for long. 'I know, and I appreciate it really. Say hi to mummy for me.'

Interesting that Grace and, presumably, Charlie didn't know of Selena's leaving. Especially when it quickly

24

became clear that lots of other people did. Minutes after this conversation with my daughter, the supportive texts started pinging in: *you all right, mate?/ Fancy a beer soon?/ If you need a natter you know where I am/ chin up, son,* all that.

People say men don't talk, but I don't think that's quite right. My experience is that there's some stuff blokes love to talk about. Scandal. Juice. Dirt. We love a bit of that. There's no gossip like a male gossip. Well, I wasn't giving them anything to chew on. They hadn't earned the right. I hadn't seen any of them for weeks.

I turned off my mobile and unplugged the landline. I couldn't be doing with heart-to-hearts or manly chats. I didn't want a shoulder to cry on. I didn't think I had the strength to withstand any sympathy right then. Maybe later there would be time for that but here's what I was going to do instead of ringing up anyone for any therapeutic whingeing: I'd have a beer or three – on my own, on a Monday, how daring is that? I'd watch an old movie. Maybe more than one. Try and make the best of things.

Selena was rarely up for watching a film. What she likes are box sets. She says the best ones are like novels. Better than novels actually because they are like books you can share, novels where you turn the pages together. I can sort of see what she means, though if Netflix box sets really are the new novels then it means that there are only ten published every year and each one is a thriller in six or thirteen chapters featuring abducted children, butchered women or both.

I decided that tonight I would read an actual novel, one with actual pages made of actual paper. A story told via the medium of dead trees. Yeah, I'd do that. I'd read a decent chunk of Larsson rather than just getting through a few pages before falling asleep. How long since I read a book when I wasn't knackered? Had been a while. Or maybe I'd play the music of my youth. Something exquisitely mindless. Something beautifully loud. Hanoi Rocks? No, the Ramones. Yes, maybe it was a Ramones kind of a night.

I didn't actually do any of these things in the end. Not really. Yes, I skim-read a couple of pages, yes, I found a film and yes – later – I put some music on, but what I really spent the evening doing was wandering the byways of the internet, seeing what friends and acquaintances were up to.

It's a funny thing about social media. You can be doing something you love – reading *The Girl With The Dragon Tattoo*, watching *The Big Sleep*, listening to punk with the volume all the way up – you can have turned your notifications off, you can be really properly immersed in something great and then, somehow, you'll get an itch to check Facebook or Twitter or Instagram or one of the other platforms where people hang out to tell each other how marvellous their lives are. It really is an itch, too. A scab you find yourself compelled to pick at. So you click on despite knowing for an absolute fact that anything you see will only irritate you.

Sometimes, despite yourself, you post about your own life, and that always, *always* makes you feel a bit sick. Bragging, even in the mildest of ways, always makes the bragger feel small. That's a lesson we learn in nursery. One it seems we have to keep on learning. Those who boast are masochists; addicts trying to get a fix of self-loathing.

I started with Selena's accounts (she hadn't posted anything) and then the kids' (nothing from them either) but then I spent hours – literally hours – clicking on the timelines of friends, almost friends, former friends, their friends, and their friends too. I scrolled through the posts of colleagues, ex-colleagues and ex-classmates.

What did I discover from all this scrolling? Nothing new. Nothing interesting. I found that everyone on Facebook was doing brilliantly, and everyone on Twitter was doing brilliantly too though they were also pretty cross about stuff. Meanwhile, over on Instagram, they were taking the trouble to actually show us all just how brilliantly they were doing. And all those pictures of trees and doorways, what does it mean?

I remember reading somewhere that three-quarters of all the photos ever taken were taken in the last three years. Mental. All of us know we're being used, being mined for data, being sold to advertisers who micro-target us to buy shit we don't need and can't afford. Or to make us elect people who should be in jail rather than in office, and still we do it at the expense of time spent doing things we love.

We should tax social media out of existence like we're doing with fags. We should health warning it to death. Pictures of hideous self-harm wounds should pop up every time you activate the relevant app. It's more likely to go the other way, though. In the future it'll be illegal not to register for all the sites. People will be required to post a minimum amount every week or you'll be charged with social media evasion. The assumption will be that only criminals try to restrict their digital footprint.

Governments love social media. No need for the Stasi to employ real humans when the citizens are busy building files on themselves: Hey, Big Brother! Look at me! No, here! I'm over here! Check me out! Look at the crazy stuff I believe! Look at the three main people who want to fuck me!

Yeah. We're fools. Slaves. All of us. Everyone. Without a shadow. Giving away our attention and our precious time for a handful of smiley faces. Pathetic.

*   *   *

27

Somehow, it was two in the morning and I'd more or less run out of alcohol – not just beer, the wine had gone too. I was drinking Advocaat because that's all there was and I updated my own status.

Everything is marvellous, everything is great. Absolutely tippetty-top and Fandabadozy. Don't you worry your pretty little heads about me.

I got a Like less than a second later.

A second after that, a comment: *Hang in there, mate.* I felt myself well up. The comment was from Doug Fairbrother. Lives in Kendal. Runs a micro-brewery. I last saw him in 1979. Doug was in the school cross-country team. Was lean and fast then, is bald and fat now. But remote as he was, even Doug Fairbrother spotted hurt behind my words. It was too much.

The second comment was from my dad. *Stay strong, lad. Dunkirk spirit.* Which meant that Selena had talked to him. Probably before she spoke to me. I could imagine how that conversation went.

Don't say anything yet, Mike, let me talk to him first.

Of course, love. Remember, you'll always be welcome here. Far as I'm concerned, you'll always be one of the family.

Thanks, Mike. Means a lot.

Something like that. Dad had always loved Selena. Called her the daughter he never had but always wanted. I guess it's lucky for me that parents don't get to pick sides after a split. Given a choice Mike Greenwood might well be one of those choosing Team Selena over Team Luke.

I deleted the post. Logged off.

I thought about watching some porn – the other per-vasive, endlessly free distraction of our age – a solace on other occasions when Selena's been gone for a night or two – but even drunk, even at 2am, the idea was too depressing. To be fifty-eight and getting myself off to the

28

adventures of Magdalene St Michaels or any similar modern-day Fanny Hill on the day my partner of thirty years left me . . . well, I may have been pissed but I was still self-aware enough to think that would be horribly sad. Sadder than sad. There has to be a limit, and Advocaat and self-pitying posts in the small hours would seem to be it.

5

SWD

'Thing is, Luke, it's not personal. You're one of many, part of a trend. Just a statistic.'

We were in The Swan, a time-warp boozer where the lights are autopsy bright, the beer tastes of metal and the air smells of pickled onion Monster Munch. There were thirty-year-old power ballads on the jukebox and football on screens in every corner. Portuguese Primeira Liga. Sporting v Braga. It's very much a one-star pub, to be honest, but I like it. We were the only people in and Dr Zoe was delivering a bit of a lecture about marital relations in the early twenty-first century.

We were having a works night out, one of a handful I've had with my staff over the years.

It may have been Zoe's idea, but the trigger was Ken or, rather, my reaction to him earlier in the day. He'd come in about twelve, asked for foie gras and quails' eggs – which was weak even for him – and I'd told him to get to fuck. He could have toast if he wanted but this time he was going to bloody pay. And it'd cost him £2.95 – which was a figure I'd just made up off the top of my head.

He looked absolutely stricken and of course I felt rubbish then. Tried to row back, to play the game like we'd always done before, but it didn't work. Ken just drew himself up to his full height – which was the first time I noticed that he was pretty tall for an older bloke – and he announced that he wouldn't be patronising what he called 'this establishment' any longer. Told us we could look forward to his Chip review which he assured us would not be favourable. Told us that maybe we'd get a visit from the Food Standards Agency too and God knows what horrors they'd find.

Zoe had stepped in. 'Come on, Ken, sling your hook. We'll see you tomorrow,' and he allowed her to lead him to the door.

When he'd shuffled off through the drizzle, she stalked over to where I was sitting in Paperwork Corner, my head in my hands.

'Bit harsh, boss.'

'Yeah, I know. I'm just—'

'We should go out.' She cut me off, her voice emphatic.

'What?'

'Me, you and Wes. Tonight. SWD.'

'What?'

'Spontaneous Works Do. Few beers. A bit of a laugh. Let off steam. Put the world to rights. Get to be the real us for a while. The people behind the aprons. You – you in particular, Mister – you so need a night out. You need to stop . . .'

'Stop what?'

Her eyes twinkled. 'You need to stop being so bloody divorceable.'

I took an executive decision not to rise to it.

'Wes will never go for a works night out.'

Only, Wes had gone for it. So there we were in The Swan with Zoe telling us about where middle-aged men and women were at.

She told us how almost every divorce these days was initiated by the woman and how more and more married

31

women were getting to fifty-odd, kids off their hands, and thinking, is that it? Is that all there is?

'They've given the best years of their lives to their husbands and their kids and their jobs, and they look at the boring, balding git they're married to, the bloke sitting on his fat, ever-spreading backside falling asleep in front of *Match of the Day* and they think, fuck this, I'm worth more than this, I'm off while there's still time to do something for myself. You can't blame them.'

'Thanks for that, Zoe,' I said.

'You're very welcome.'

'I don't even like *Match of the Day*.'

She smiled. Zoe is so frowny generally that when she smiles it's like the sun coming out. Makes people near her feel cheery and warm whatever she's just said. She has a smile that's contagious. She should deploy it more. Despite myself, I smiled back.

'There's probably someone else anyway,' said Wes.

'What?' I said.

'There usually is,' said Wes. 'In my experience.'

'That's ridiculous.'

Wes shrugged, stood up and announced that he needed a slash. I saw Zoe shoot him a look. Not one I could read. Wes shrugged again, just a twitch of the shoulders really, and I couldn't read that either.

You'll think I'm an idiot but it hadn't occurred to me that Selena was having an affair. It just wasn't like her. In the past whenever talk about someone cheating had come up in conversation, Selena had always been unforgiving. Never any excuse for it. That was always her line.

Zoe was talking again. Steamrolling on as if Wes hadn't said anything. 'You should see this as a wake-up call, Luke. You should use it as an opportunity to really change your own life.'

32

On she went, repeating in a dozen different ways that the break-up was actually brilliant news for all concerned. A blessing in disguise.

'Thing is, Luke. All change is good.'

'So says the history PhD who has spent the last four years serving up tea to brickies.'

She ignored this. She wasn't going to be deflected. 'Anyway, I know this for sure: if you really want to get Selena back you need to become interesting again. You need to become surprising somehow. And maybe you should get some new clothes and a haircut. See a dentist.'

There was more like this, with all her words stumbling out in a hurry. She barely took a gulped half-breath between sentences. She was like someone trying to explain herself to a policeman. It didn't matter though because I was hardly listening. I was trying to text Selena with fingers grown suddenly clumsy and hard to operate.

Is there someone else?

I chucked my phone on the formica of the pub table and came back to what Zoe was saying just as she suggested I should take an evening class. Meet some new friends.

'Why?' I said. 'Because all the *old* friends will be on Selena's side?'

'Luke, it's not about sides. But yes, I guess. Most people will see more of her because I bet Selena has put the effort in. She's invested all the emotional labour. She's nurtured the friendships.'

'And you know this how, exactly?'

Now Zoe shrugged. 'That's the dynamic, isn't it? That's just how men and women are in relationships.'

'Not in this particular case,' I said, pompously and, also, untruthfully. I bloody well wasn't about to admit it, but yes, I suppose it was Selena that arranged

33

get-togethers, who sent cards and presents, who remembered birthdays and who we owed dinners. Selena who popped round to see people who were ill or a bit depressed. Selena who went to groups and classes and who chatted with people at the end of them. Selena who had work friends and yoga friends and badminton friends and school-gate friends that she met when the kids were smaller and had hung on to.

It was definitely Selena who did the emotional heavy lifting with Dad after my mother died. Nevertheless, it was galling that Zoe could just say this so blithely, like it was some kind of Natural Law. Men are like this, woman are like that – Venus, Mars, etc. – it was annoying. And no less annoying just because in this instance it happened to be true.

'Well, you're all right then, aren't you?' she said.

She took the time to explain that she agreed with me actually: men aren't from Mars. They're from Pluto. A cold and desolate rock that isn't really worthy of being called a planet. And women? Women aren't just from Venus. Women are from all the planets. Women are the whole universe and everything.

There was the jolly little ding of an incoming text. We both looked at my phone as it winked and shivered on the table among the glasses. I picked it up. I was dimly aware of Wes arriving back from the toilet, of Zoe and him exchanging looks again. This time her look was very readable. It's a look that called Wes a twat. His answering look was confused, almost hurt.

Selena's text: *There is someone I've got close to.*

We drank up in silence. No one suggested another round. We all knew this SWD was over and that it had been an experiment that wouldn't be repeated for a while.

34

6

WHY SHOULD WE BE BETTER THAN THAT?

I was singing at the top of my voice, lost in the crack in the space-time continuum that the music of your youth opens up. I was playing the first Clash album. I was fifty-eight but I was also fifteen. I was in my lounge, but I was also back in my bedroom in Gaitskell Close in 1978 and also in all the other places where that band had kept me company. I was wearing nothing but my pants.

Selena tapped me on the shoulder and I jumped out of my skin. She laughed and yes, I could see how it had looked a bit comical. A grown man, more or less naked, playing air guitar and pogo-ing. It was definitely embarrassing, but people shouldn't sneak around in houses that they've left. Not good manners. Not playing the game.

She gestured for me to turn the music down and when I'd done that, when my fifteen-year-old self had slunk away, taking all my other past selves with him, when the shimmering ghost layers of other rooms had vanished, she said that I might want to put on more clothes. She didn't need to say this. At that moment I was very conscious of my lumpy whiteness, the varicosed flesh that somehow managed to be both scrawny and flabby simultaneously.

Selena was the first girl to make me feel that it didn't matter what I looked like when I took my shirt off, that

35

taking my shirt off would generally always be a worth-while thing whatever the state of my chest, shoulders, stomach. Well, those days were gone forever now. Self-consciousness was back and its nasty little fingers were handling all the stuff in my head. Spreading germs into all my thoughts.

When I was dressed, when I'd taken the record off – you don't have serious break-up talks with The Clash as background music – when we were sitting down facing each other, I asked how she was. She shrugged and told me that she was signed off work for two weeks. Stress.

It was true that she didn't look well. She was tired, pale, thin. I studied the lines on her face, the shadows beneath her eyes, the new crow's feet.

I could do this – stare at her without her calling me on it – because she was looking anywhere rather than at me. She looked at the living room as if she was seeing it for the first time. As if she was wondering where these curtains came from and was that really the carpet we chose? As if it wasn't how she remembered it, as if it contained surprises. She looked at it like she was a nostalgic visitor to a place dimly remembered, like when you go back to your primary school and it all seems smaller than it should be. How could you ever have got your knees under that desk? All that.

At this point she had been gone all of ten days.

'Place is pretty tidy,' she said.

'Why wouldn't it be?'

'Did you get a cleaner in?'

I could have denied it, I suppose. Could have acted all affronted. Could have chosen to start a fight there and then: you think I can't work a hoover? You think I can't load a dishwasher? But I didn't have the energy, and anyway Selena knew me too well.

'Yeah,' I said. 'Fiona from Dusters.'

She smiled now. A sad little smile accompanied by a nod to herself as if getting Fiona from Dusters in to do what I didn't have time to do myself was some kind of moral failing, as if it confirmed a truth about my basic inadequacy. So I was irritated, which was good because it's impossible to be emotionally devastated by someone who is also getting on your tits.

She wanted to talk about the children. She wanted me to have a word with them. Apparently they weren't speaking to her. She'd taken over a week to let them know how things stood between us and now they didn't answer her calls or messages. I was cheered to hear this – of course I was – and then slightly ashamed of myself.

Thing was, I had been hearing from the kids. They worried about me. Was I eating? Was I looking after myself? Charlie in particular phoned every day, more or less. Maybe I was reaping the reward of all those freezing Sunday mornings spent on the touchlines cheering him on while he chased rugby balls through mud and frost.

Or maybe it went back further, to when he was a tiny tot prone to waking at night because of furniture turning into shadowy monsters in the night. Those times in the early hours where I read him stories about little bears while his moth-breath fluttered warm against my chest.

Selena used to say that I was colluding in his wakefulness, that I rewarded his disturbing our nights by turning them into special dad-and-son times, leaving her to be the moany, tired and grouchy parent who had to go to work feeling like shit. Whatever the reason – maybe Charlie was just particularly sceptical of my ability to cope – he'd been particularly caring. He's a good kid.

'I don't hear from them much either,' I lied. 'They're busy and they're thoughtless. They're students. There's probably some vital no-platforming to do. Or children's

TV to watch. They might even be in the library. It's a possibility at least.'

Selena said this was different. Kids just not being in touch with their parents unless they want money or favours, well, yeah that's normal, but not returning calls or texts at all? Hanging up when you do finally get through – which you can only do when you call from a borrowed mobile or from an unfamiliar landline? Something else is going on then.

'They're angry and things they took for granted as unbreakable have turned out to be fragile. They'll get over it.' I paused for a beat. 'Maybe.' I couldn't help myself.

Meanwhile I was thinking, *whose borrowed mobile? Whose landline?*

'Yeah, maybe,' she said.

She looked wretched in a way I hadn't ever seen before. This annoyed me. *Well, boo-hoo, Selena, you've made your bed.* But, as we stumbled through a conversation where she told me I looked well and I responded in kind – and both of us were lying – I found myself thawing. She seemed so thoroughly miserable and though I sort of wanted that, I also sort of didn't. Selena feeling crap made me feel crap. It always had and I found I couldn't really bring myself to luxuriate in her misery now. I was too much in the habit of wanting the best for her. I said that I'd talk to them.

'Thanks,' she said. 'I'd appreciate that.' A lukewarm response which irritated me all over again.

While she got her stuff together I made another coffee and tried to ignore the sound of movement in the bedroom above, those significant creaks, those meaningful thumps and bumps. I tried not to guess which drawers were being opened, or to imagine the rummaging through clothes – the selection of some, the rejection of others depending on how well they would fit her new life.

I put another record on: First Aid Kit. We both loved them. Went to see them together whenever they came this way. Something we shared. Maybe I was hoping those voices blending together in harmony would trigger something in her. I didn't know what that thing might be exactly. Nostalgia that would trigger remorse that would fire up affection and wanting to get back together? Some tidy little chain reaction like that? Maybe. Or maybe it was punishment I was trying to inflict. Look at what you've thrown away, all the music we've shared – it's going to hurt you now.

She didn't take long in the bedroom. The album was still on side one when Selena came downstairs. She had two suitcases, both of them dusty – we'd been travelling hand luggage only for so long that our bigger suitcases had been sitting out of sight, out of mind on top of the wardrobe for years.

'I don't know what you're going to do with all your stuff when you're in a smaller house,' she said.

This remark was so cold that it hit me like a kick in the guts. 'Why will I be in a smaller house?' I said. 'In fact why will I be in any other house?'

'Oh, God, Luke, surely we're not going to fight over money and property, are we? I thought we'd be better than that.'

Why? Why should we better than that? Why should we be better than anyone?

'Okay,' I said. 'Let's not fight about the house.'

'Good,' she said.

'Let's fight about your cheating,' I said.

Her eyes flashed. 'I don't want to get into this now.'

'But you do want me to help you re-establish relation-ships with our children.'

She sighed. 'What do you really want to know, Luke?'

'The usual. Who, what, where, how and why. All of it. Everything.'

'Everything? Seriously?'

I waited.

She took a breath. Geared herself up to answer, and I felt panic rising. I wanted to call the words back. Turned out I didn't want to know everything. Fact, I didn't want to know anything. Once I'd got the information I'd have to do something with it.

This is why I was such a terrible journalist in the end. I never really wanted there to be any news, and if there was any I wanted someone else to have to deal with it.

What, where, who, how and why. These are the questions you are taught to ask in journalism – but actually only one of them is interesting. The why. This is given the least importance in news reports and yet it is the only thing that really matters. But it was too late to reverse now. I'd asked for it and now I was going to get it. All of it.

The cold ins and the outs. We all know them. Anyone who has ever glanced at a magazine or accidentally watched a TV soap knows them. Anyone who has ever had a job knows them. The banality of the inappropriate workplace romance is almost embarrassing.

It begins with innocuous work chat: deadlines, the idiocy of senior management, inbox overload. It continues with banter in the staff kitchen or at the photocopier, small talk about your home life that becomes progressively more intimate. *The thing about Luke is . . . It really winds me up when he . . .* The sympathetic, half-whispered replies: *I know what you mean, my missus is exactly the same . . .*

Coffee breaks taken together. Then lunches, then being – somehow – the last two in the office. Drinks after

work and dinners after the drinks until, step by predictable step it leads, almost inevitably, to weekends away, to
declarations of love, to plans to leave homes, spouses,
children. Sometimes these plans are even acted on. Zoe
was right, such a depressingly ordinary story. The lazi-
ness was the most disheartening thing, I think; that she
couldn't be bothered to look any further than the hot
desk next to hers. I never thought my wife would be lazy,
not in anything.

In Selena's case she swore there was just the one weekend away and it came right at the end. In Whitby, she
said, as though the location mattered. As though it would
have been a worse betrayal if it had been somewhere
bigger and more obviously glitzy. It's not like it was Paris,
she seemed to be saying. Not somewhere really exciting,
but also, you know, not a Travelodge in Milton Keynes
either, which would be equally disgraceful for other reasons. Reasons of taste.

'Fish and chips in Whitby. How lovely,' I said. 'That
would be the weekend where you said you were going
on a spa break with some of the girls from work.'

I knew what I sounded like. I sounded bitter and
mean. Spiteful. But I'd earned the right. She sighed. She
was on a roll now, couldn't stop, so I learned her lover's
name – Jacob Mandel – and his job. He was some kind of
IT whizz, which actually meant nothing because doesn't
everyone do something in IT these days?

Over the next ten minutes I learned way too much about
this bloody Jacob. Facts about Selena's lover were bundled
up without sense or thought, the way her clothes were in
those too hastily packed suitcases. I learned that he was
six foot two. That he loved rock-climbing and mountain-
biking. That he joined her firm a year ago. That he played
football on Sundays. That he was close to his mum and
his sisters, like that tells you anything about anyone.

41

I learned that Selena didn't even like him at first. Didn't trust him. Thought he was too loud, too sure of himself. I learned that he spoke French, did a gap year working in a high-end fish restaurant in Lyon. Who cares? I thought. Who gives a monkey's about his gap year? But I couldn't get her to stop telling me stuff. I tried, but it was impossible.

She said that he just brought fun into her life at a time when she needed it. Then fun became something else. She didn't think it would mean anything but. She stopped there. She shrugged. The amount of shrugging people did when I talked to them. And sighing. Shrugging and sighing. Pissed me off, frankly.

Anyway, she was powerless, she said. It was hopeless. She was helpless. In the grip of something bigger than herself. She did try to fight it. Tried to break it off several times.

She ended by saying he reminded her of me actually. Of how I used to be anyway. Which also pissed me off. Made me snappish.

'Oh, yeah? And how did I used to be?'

She shrugged again. I kept my temper. Well done me.

'I don't know, more fun. Happier maybe. You wanted to do more. To see more people. You were more curious about things and people. Also, you weren't . . .'

'Weren't what?'

'Nothing.'

'No, come on. I can take it. Weren't what?'

She sighed. Looked at the ceiling. I knew what was coming. And, yep, there it was. A little what-the-hell shrug. All this fucking shrugging. It was going to do me in.

'You weren't as out of shape. Weren't as fat. You've let yourself go, Luke. It's a fact. Actually, I think you might be depressed, but I've realised there's nothing I can do

42

about that. It's not my job and I can't let you pull me down with you. I have to save my own life.'

Why did I ask these things? Why did I insist on the truth like this? It's always a mistake. Maybe it was thanks to some long-buried but hard-to-shake-off journalistic reflex. Still, I was taken aback by her need to get everything out there. The most hurtful thing was that it was clear that she wasn't saying anything to wound. She was in love with this Jacob and she wanted to tell the world. Had to tell the world. Everyone had to get to hear about it. Must have been driving her work colleagues mad.

There was something nagging at me though, something else I wanted to ask. But I had to wait. She told me about how awkward it had been at work, even though colleagues and friends had been great about everything, considering. She couldn't have survived without them. Waited while she told me about meeting up with Jacob's mum and sisters and how they were lovely. I waited while she said that it was only our kids that didn't seem to understand. They didn't seem to cut her any slack at all.

It was only after all this, when she finally paused for breath, that I could ask my question.

'How old is this guy, Selena?'

That shut her up.

She flushed. Looked suddenly feverish. She pushed her hand through her hair. Looked at the floor. First Aid Kit finished their thing and the silence in the room was very loud.

'Twenty-six.' Her voice was a whisper. A defiant whisper, but a whisper nevertheless. She smiled, but it was watery. 'I know. What am I doing?'

Just then, just at that moment, I wasn't angry with her. I wanted to hold her.

I didn't though. I looked at my hands. They were shaking. The house smelled a bit cabbagy. Maybe I should get Fiona from Dusters in again. I raised my head and met her eyes. She gave me another bleak smile, wet eyes wide in some kind of appeal, and I felt close to her suddenly, but I didn't know what she was asking me for, just that whatever it was I couldn't supply it. I offered her more tea instead. Her smile flickered again and she said no, she'd better get going. I carried those two dusty suitcases out to her car. They weren't heavy. In fact they seemed to weigh almost nothing.

7

OUTSIDE CATERING

I was in a big house in one of those chocolate boxy North Yorkshire villages. Easeby is a place that was often used as a set when TV still made those cosy Sunday teatime dramas. Stone cottages. Narrow cobbled streets. Urchins in caps and knickerbockers. Family feuds. Illegitimate children, disinherited heiresses. Sex offending sons of the local gentry. You know the kind of thing. The shows that depressed you as a kid because it meant the weekend was almost done and yet another grey treadmill of school days was about to start.

Easeby is pretty close to *Heartbeat*, not far from *Last of the Summer Wine*, just around the corner from *Emmerdale*. Its current beamed and mullioned appearance concealing a dark past. This is a village that continued to burn witches long after everyone else had moved on, a place where the local Lord of the Manor exercised *droit du seigneur* until about 1985, if Wikipedia is to be believed. It has changed: the manor house is a conference centre now and the past torture of women is only nodded at in the name of the pub – The Ducking Stool – but it feels like there's still something sinister lurking in these coach party friendly cobbled streets. Some weird chill in the air.

I was there to talk to a Mrs Hobbs about catering for a party. Outside catering was not something we did as a regular thing but it could be a useful additional income stream.

Mrs Hobbs showed me around a large and well-proportioned, skilfully renovated seventeenth-century farmhouse. She was a well-groomed lady of indeterminate age. Elderly but still athletic-looking. Tennis or golf or horse riding or all three. Dancing too maybe. Samba in the village hall on Thursdays. There was probably Pilates in the mix somewhere. Personally supervised and bespoke stretching of some kind anyway.

She was sceptical about me. Without saying a critical word she managed to hint pretty strongly that getting Team Ernies in to do dawn fry-ups for the last of the revellers wasn't her idea. When she first opened the door she had looked me up and down – not in a sexual way, don't get me wrong – more in a buying a dog sort of a way. Could I fetch a shot partridge? Could I catch a rabbit? Bait a badger? Was my coat glossy? Were my teeth capable of crunching a bone?

Her expression was both sharp and resigned. She expected the world to try and get one over on her and it got her down sometimes. Still, she made a decent brew in a kitchen that was considerably larger than the one we had in Ernies and we got chatting a bit.

'Important do, this party?' I said.

'It would seem so,' she said.

Turned out that her own fiftieth wedding anniversary, her youngest daughter's fortieth birthday and her husband's eightieth all fell on the same weekend. She said that if it was up to her she'd just go to The Ducking Stool for a dinner with the husband and pay for the daughter to host her own do in town, but it wasn't how Mr Hobbs liked to do things. He liked the big gesture, the grand statement. Speeches and toasts. Free breakfasts for his guests as the sun rises. Couldn't do anything by halves.

Having confided her feelings about the party and given me this small insight into her home life, she thawed out a little more while giving me the tour of the house. Asked me to call her Margaret for a start.

'"Mrs Hobbs" makes me feel so old,' she said.

You're arranging a fortieth birthday party for your youngest daughter, I thought. It's your own fiftieth wedding anniversary. No getting away from it, Mrs Hobbs – Margaret – you are quite old.

It was an attractive house. Tastefully decorated in an uncluttered style. Clean lines, lots of apple-white. Lots of light. I liked it. Made me want to have a thorough clear-out when I got back home. I made sure I praised it.

'Very Nordic,' I said. 'Very now.'

It was the right thing to say and she talked me through her thinking, how she removed a dividing wall between the kitchen and dining room to create a large open-plan living space with views over the moors. How they had turned the old workshops into the kitchen, filling in the gap with a dining and sitting area with an apex roof that linked to a new extension. The extension itself was a multi-purpose space big enough to host parties, even extravagant ones.

She told me that she would have liked to do interior design professionally as a career maybe. I said she still could and she made a face. No, really, I said. I told her that I had it on good authority that older women were taking over. That they were the future, actually. There was a revolution happening, I said. She could be part of it.

She seemed unconvinced. I felt I'd made a misstep somehow.

'Have you had lunch?' I said.

There and then I made her a simple mushroom ome-lette. The secret is a little fresh finely chopped green chilli in with the mushrooms, a dash of soy sauce and a blob of good double cream in with the egg mixture. I served it with sautéed potatoes. Wes might do the day-to-day work in the kitchen at Ernies but I can still do the show-boat stuff if I have to.

It worked anyway. Did what it should. Hard to resist the perfect omelette. Margaret Hobbs ended up offering me an insane amount of money for the gig. We would get the same for doing this party as we would for a month just slogging away in the caff. For some reason I felt I had to protest.

'It's too much.'

Margaret begged to differ. We bickered good-naturedly and pointlessly for a few minutes, both of us aware of the absurdity of the customer trying to raise the price, the supplier trying to lower it. It was a game, one she finally put a stop to.

'Look, Luke, my husband has done very well for himself. Very well indeed when you consider what he came from: two rooms in Stonebeck. Mother left when he was seven. His father was always out of work and generally drunk. Violent too.'

It was a classic boy-made-good story. Dickensian stuff. Hobbs basically brought himself up. Grafted hard, ducked and dived, bobbed and weaved and now he lived here in this fine old house, with his wife whose own father had been Mayor of Leeds back in the day.

They had other houses too, of course. A place in Portugal and a place in Jersey. Tony drove a vintage Jensen Interceptor. Margaret had a nippy little baby Merc. They had horses. Kids both went to private schools and, despite managing to leave those incredibly expensive establishments with barely a GCSE between them, they also had nice houses, big cars, lovely holidays, all paid for by Tony's grafting.

She told me she could have whatever she wanted. 'Tony's always asking me to buy more things. Clothes, shoes, stuff for the house, trips abroad. Art. He gets annoyed when he gets the credit card statements and finds out I haven't used them. It winds him up.' She laughed as she told me that whenever she was pissed off with him she simply refused to spend money. 'If I'm in a real sulk I can go months without buying anything. Drives him crazy.'

She said that Tony also liked to think he was still down to earth. 'That's another reason why he wants you,' she said. 'He loves the idea of a business based in the same slums he escaped from, serving food to the local nobs.'

I bristled at the casual use of the word *slums*. I was allowed to call them that. This Margaret was emphatically not. Not with that gymkhana accent.

Sharp-eyed as she was, she noticed. 'Tony's words, not mine.'

Her point was that she wanted her husband to feel this party would go with a proper swing, that it would be like some Yorkshire rewrite of *The Great Gatsby*, so she had to make sure she'd paid over the odds for everything. Tony Hobbs was one of those people who only feel they've got the best if they've spent eye-watering sums of cash. If it doesn't cost big-league, then how do you know it even matters?

'Anyway,' she said at last. 'You should see what the band are getting and they're shit.'

She smiled as I recoiled from the unexpected oath. It was the reaction she'd hoped for.

There was a soft cough and we looked up and discovered we were being watched. A tough-looking man in early middle age, a bloke just beginning to show the effects of time's steady vandalism. Reddening skin, thickening waist, thinning hair shaved close to the skull, mean eyes in a pudgy face. He looked like he might still enjoy a ruck on the terraces. A scrap on a Saturday.

We nodded at each other. He looked familiar, but one thing I've noticed about getting older is that everyone starts to look a bit familiar, though placing where you met them gets harder. That bloke running the news-agents? You might have sat next to him in double history for five years. That woman drinking with her friends in the pub? Could be an old work colleague. Could be a friend of your wife's. Could be the ex-wife of your best mate. Or she could be a stranger who just happens to resemble a sitcom actress from the 1980s. Someone who once had a cameo in *Only Fools and Horses*.

Routine face-blindness is like varicose veins, another small humiliation inflicted by advancing age. It was actually Zoe who taught me the proper name for it: prosopagnosia. She says the whole country is afflicted with it because English people don't like to look very closely at anything – including faces – in case they see something that frightens them.

'This is my son-in-law, Micky,' said Margaret. 'Works with Tony. Married to Joanie, our youngest.'

There was no warmth in her voice. I got the impression that she had never considered this Micky much of an addition to the family, that she had always thought of her Joanie's marriage to him as not so much gaining a son but very much losing a daughter.

'How do,' he said. His voice was toneless and thin.

'All right,' I said.

It's fair to say that we didn't take to each other. If I'd met Micky before, it wasn't anywhere good.

Halfway back to the city and I was overwhelmed by dread. I had to pull off the motorway onto the hard shoulder. I had to take a few deep breaths. Try and calm down. This happened sometimes. It had happened before Selena left too, though not as often. The sudden

50

realisation that one day – quite soon in the scheme of things – I'll be dead. We all will. Selena, Charlie, Grace, Zoe, Wes, the fucker Jacob, all our friends, everyone we've ever loved. All ashes and dust. Carbonised dandruff.

It's senseless because it shouldn't matter. The world managed quite well without me for several hundred millennia, and I don't miss all those years. Time travel would be fun and everything, but I'm not poleaxed with grief because I missed the birth of rock and roll, or the Battle of Trafalgar or the Black Death. Why should I worry any more about being absent for all the possible futures than I do about missing all the past that's been and gone?

It's not that I fear the process of dying either. The National Health Service is good at death. It's a thing it does well. As a rule we're helped to slip out of this vale of tears helpfully – even beautifully – medicated, a softly smiling nurse (and in my imagination, very beautiful, probably from one of the Mediterranean countries, sun-ripened skin made glowing by great salads, by olives, by decent wine) promising to make us *more comfortable* as she proffers the needle, as she slides in the spike. And if it's not like this – if our end is shocking, brutal and painful, if we go hard, coughing out our last seconds on the damp concrete of some drab street somewhere – well, then at least it'll probably be quick.

No, it's not really the fact of death that gets me; it's just horror at how fast life has gone. A minute ago I was a kid. Seconds ago, I was buying a flat, seconds after that Selena was moving in, then there was a house, then the kids were busy being born. Took no time at all. In a few seconds more it'll be my funeral. A few old men at the wake, good bacon sarnies served because it's what I would have wanted. Something noisy but melodic on the stereo as my coffin slides behind that grubby municipal curtain and into the grubby municipal oven.

51

What I really want is to live forever. For my children to live forever. If there has to be change, any change at all, then it should be slow and should always be for the better. Not too much to ask, is it?

I guess you could call it a panic attack, though that seems a banal phrase for the absolute swamping sickness of it. A kind of epilepsy of the heart is what it is. A haemorrhage in the soul. For a few minutes I just have to stop whatever I'm doing and sit and weep. Sob like a child lost in dark woods without his parents.

I didn't snap out of it, either. No, I had to haul myself out of the funk inch by desperate inch. Fight for a kind of sanity, like thrashing my way to the surface of a deep and freezing sea. Breath coming in wracking gulps when I finally broke through into light and air. Lungs raw.

What helped with this one was the knowledge that pretty soon the traffic police would turn up and want to ask their questions, and I had the suspicion that my reply – 'it just struck me, Officer, one day I'll be dead. And so will you, and isn't that fucking obscene?' – might not cut the mustard. Might get me banged up, if not in the nick then in a psychiatric ward somewhere.

When I did get it together to drive on to Ernies I found the troops unimpressed by news that we'd landed a lucrative outside catering gig. Zoe told me that she'd have to consult her social calendar.

'I might find that one of The Three is taking me out to try and get in my knickers.'

Wes snorted at this, and then grunted that he'd make a pie or summat, but don't expect him to go all the way to North Yorkshire to serve it at daybreak.

'Brilliant. Thanks a million. Appreciate all the enthusiasm,' I said.

'You know what they say about sarcasm,' said Zoe. 'It's the stupid man's idea of cleverness.'

Anyway, the troops had news of their own. While I was gone there had been a party of guys in suits, at least five of them, taking pictures of the place. Photos of both the inside and the outside. Wes had to chase a guy out of the kitchen.

'All very weird,' said Zoe.

I was thinking it wasn't weird at all. I was thinking Ken, the old bastard, he did it. He actually got it together to complain to the city council and they had sent their crack food hygiene squad in. Well, good luck to them. Whatever the one-star reviewers said – and there had been more of them recently – Wes always had the place immaculate, the kitchen of Ernies was always as sterile as a mortuary. We had nothing to fear from that department.

Zoe had other news too. 'Oh, and your missus came in.'

'Selena?'

'Unless you have another wife I don't know about.'

'What did she want?'

'To see you, I guess.'

'Why didn't you call me?'

Zoe just looked at me, rolled her eyes.

'Yeah, sorry.' I said.

Over the last couple of weeks I'd been mislaying my phone and when I did have it on me it seemed to be more or less permanently out of charge. I swear it wasn't delib- erate but I can see how it could look like it was. When my phone rang or pinged it was either someone asking how I was, or it was Selena wanting to deal with those bloody practicalities – solicitors and estate agents and all that. She'd got very fierce and focused since I failed to convince the kids to be kinder to her. I did try, phoned them both the day Selena came round to get her stuff but they were

53

both too angry to entertain the idea of speaking to her. I didn't really push it, to be honest.

It wasn't just my phone I'd been neglecting. I'd also avoided Facebook and Twitter and any WhatsApp groups I'd accidentally found myself a part of. When I wasn't at work I wanted to be alone with my real friends – my movies, my music, my books. Booze. Food.

I was ghosting everyone. Ghosting the whole goddam world. Not that the whole goddam world had really noticed.

I asked if I could borrow Zoe's phone. As she handed it over she tried to reassure me.

'She looked all right, you know. She was friendly actually. Cheerful. I think she probably just wants to check in, to keep things nice. She might even be worried about you.'

'She'll be wanting her money from the house,' said Wes. 'Half your pension too, probably.'

'Oh, Wes,' Zoe said and laughed. Her eyes sparkled. She flicked a tea towel at him. 'What are you like?'

After we shut, after Zoe and Wes had gone, I sat in Paperwork Corner in the dark. Going home just seemed like too much of an effort. I got as far as loading the dishwasher and turning off the lights and it kind of wore me out. To get any further with the whole going home thing I'd have to get up, get my coat, pull the shutters down, lock the place, set the alarms – all too exhausting to even think about. Maybe I'd do it in a minute but for now I'd just drink a mug of builders amid all this defiantly eclectic furniture, most of it exquisitely uncomfortable, nearly all of it sourced by Selena. The product of hours spent going through the classifieds, and haunting auction rooms, car boots, thrift shops and eBay.

Life is all about choices and right then I chose to sit in the dark and brood. Sulk, Selena would say. Outside there was the growl of the low-geared cars nosing through the streets, voices raised in anger or distress. Shrieking of all kinds. Stonebeck is a Managed Prostitution Zone, which means managed misery and I'm not sure if this is better or worse than the unmanaged kind. Hard to say. Anyway, there was the usual bolero of slow-witted laughter. That modernist symphony of glass smashing. The inevitable sirens. The night just getting started.

Where do these people find the energy?

8

TINTIN AND THE LAST GOLDEN AGE

'We should tell everyone who has two houses or more that they need to choose the one they want to live in because we, the people, will take the spare ones and use them to house the homeless.' She was ladling soup into the polystyrene cups held out by a line of rough sleepers and explaining to me why we should ban holiday cottages and buy-to-lets. Telling me why being a landlord should be as unacceptable as being a thief. It was 20 December 1988 and we were working together at the soup kitchen she ran in the High Road. There was a fierce frost in the air and fairy lights in the windows of the kebab shops, fully tinselled-up plastic Christmas trees behind the barred windows of the houses. If I hadn't been with Selena it would have been deeply depressing.

She was twenty-one, her hair was a short boyish crop and her face was full of sharp points and flinty edges. Chin, nose, forehead, lips, teeth, cheekbones: her face looked like it was made of specialised cutting tools. Something you'd use for shaping diamonds. There was good-humoured energy in every movement of a compact body made lithe by childhood gymnastics and kept that way by five-a-side soccer and sessions at the university climbing wall.

Selena had a lot of radical opinions at that time and what was funny was how even this most disenfranchised of communities thought her views were too extreme. The homeless would say thank you for the soup and then accuse her of being a communist troublemaker.

Selena would just laugh and go on to lay some of her other beliefs on them. Her idea that inheritance tax should be increased to 100 per cent. Or that when she was General Secretary of the UK she'd introduce conscription – not to increase the supply of soldiers – she'd actually abolish the army – but to make sure we got enough teachers, nurses and social workers.

'Anyone capable of that kind of work should be made to do it for a couple of years. People would be more respectful of the public sector then,' she said.

Or she would talk about extending the principle of the jury system to Parliament. Her idea was that if we trust juries to get at the truth in criminal trials then why not have a jury of six hundred ordinary men and women sitting in Westminster to choose the laws?

Trust the people, that was her thing then. Funny thing was the people – the one she met anyway – weren't so sure they could be trusted.

The junkies, the drunks, the mentally disordered, they would shake their heads and mutter even more, genuinely alarmed now. Selena's a wild card, this head-shaking and muttering would imply, a dangerous enemy of the state. She should be locked up. This made her laugh too: how conservative you are, she would say to the bootless and the roofless, how conventional.

I was in love with her from that first day. From the first moment I saw her. I was twenty-five and had – somehow – been a reporter with *The Post* for seven years. It was the fag end of what we all now realise was a fabled

Last Golden Age of Regional Journalism, though at the time it just felt like a succession of blurred afternoons.

Hard to imagine now but in 1988 journos, even local ones, had power. Newspapers had real muscle to flex. We were encouraged – ordered even – to search around, to find out what our leaders were hiding. We were expected to lift rocks to find out what was lurking underneath, to shine lights into dark corners. Investigations took as long as they took and they cost as much as they had to. I've known colleagues spend months on solving a murder case where the police had given up after a couple of weeks. Provincial newspapers had their own parliamentary correspondents. Some even had their own foreign correspondents giving a bespoke regional spin on news from key war zones.

It's not like that now. These days a local paper – if it still exists – gets a press release and someone uploads it without even reading it. Uploading – and what an ugly word that is – seems to be the whole of the job these days.

Local paper newsrooms were different in the 1980s because newspapers really mattered then. People read them. Not only that, they walked into shops and bought them. They, you know, paid real money for them. Notes and coins. Big companies advertised in them. Everyone else advertised in them too. They had to. In a pre-eBay world, papers were where you sold your unwanted crap.

All of which meant newspapers were profitable concerns as well as being connecting glue for whole communities. And the fact they made money meant proper numbers of trained staff working for editors with a passion for the work. Editors were like warlords back then. Battle-scarred and fearless. Their word was law. A newsroom in the 1980s was like a Tudor court.

* * *

I'll fess up straight away that when I met Selena at that soup kitchen I really wasn't a good reporter. I wasn't one of the fearless tough guys speaking truth to power. I was a clock-watcher, doing the barest of minimums. Someone who had drifted into journalism because I quite liked English at school and didn't fancy going to university. I had sent in a slangy and hyperbolic review of the first *Star Wars* film on spec which somehow found its way to Nicholas Schatz MC, the sixty-five-year-old Dunkirk veteran and Assistant News Editor, which convinced him that I was the kind of hip young gunslinger he was lacking on his team.

Even top editors got it wrong sometimes.

I never wanted to be Bob Woodward or Carl Bernstein. If the newsroom phone rang, I'd move towards it in slow motion hoping that someone else would get there first. Someone usually did, but if I absolutely had to answer it I'd be praying that it was something trivial and boring, something barely worthy of a news in brief par – a nib – buried deep in the innards of the paper. A cat up a tree. A bus route alteration. I realised very early on that I wasn't war reporter material and so did everyone else.

I should have been fired really, but the old soaks who ran things then may have been fierce but they were also tolerant of uselessness as long as it wasn't ambitious. Someone who wanted to climb the greasy pole without putting the graft in would have been gone in minutes, but someone who just wanted to get paid for idling his days away? Well, they could put up with that. Respect it almost. They even devised a stratagem to help me dodge proper assignments. They encouraged me to put my faux leather jacket (purchased with my first month's wages) over one of the chairs in the newsroom and leave it there, so if I was ever asked for by the editor they could reply that I must be around somewhere, look, here's his ridiculous jacket.

They'd move that jacket around various chairs so I could spend days in record shops or at the flicks if I wanted. In return they would expect me to do the stuff they couldn't bear to do like covering parish councils, rock gigs, school plays and, especially, the 'Challenge the *Post*' feature.

'Challenge the *Post*' was where a reporter would be photographed spending a day doing the job of one of the readers and then write three hundred amusing words about it. Proper journos loathed it, but I rather liked it. It could be quite relaxing. Among the assignments I remember was my day as a colour therapist (I should wear more mustard-coloured jackets apparently, would help even up my lopsided shoulders) and a particularly good day spent as a firefighter (we washed the engine and then played table tennis the rest of the shift).

It was just after the fire engine feature appeared that we were dared to spend a night helping to run an all-night soup kitchen in the High Road.

The way old Schatz put it to me was that a gauntlet had been thrown down by a gobby final year university student called Selma Something and he thought it might make a nice Christmassy piece – a feel-good story about how our readers were a kind-hearted, generous and public-spirited lot. It might also be a possible antidote to the gloom promoted by our usual stories of drug-related robberies in broad daylight.

'I want the reek of effin jingle bells coming off your copy,' he said. 'I want cheery tramps turning cartwheels while singing hark the effin angels come. I want It's A Wonderful effin Life. Make sure you get this Selma bint in the sexy Santa suit for the pic.'

That was my battle-plan but it was derailed by discovering – less than twenty minutes in – that I was totally smitten. The Santa suit stayed in its bag and I found myself consumed with a desire to impress, which meant that for a short while I became the decent, hard-working newshound I should have been right from the beginning. My change in approach began when I filled my piece with some of Selena's choicer political maxims. None of which appeared – instead we had her described as the Saint of Stonebeck High Road which Selena found infuriating. She rang to complain which did at least give me the chance to ask her out.

'I don't think so,' she said.

I wore her down though and I'm willing to bet that it was the proliferation of bylines and scoops rather than the Happy Hour cocktails, bogof pizzas or the Playhouse tickets that helped wean her off her boyfriend of the time. He was the uni badminton captain then. Now he's a Labour MP, I think. Not a front-bench one, but still.

During the months it took to complete this mission I worked harder than I've ever worked. I was first to the office, first to the phone, I went through my contacts book asking for stories, poring through minutes of local authority planning meetings looking for things the council were trying to get past us. Volunteering for extra shifts in court. I became, in the words of Nicholas Schatz, 'a right effin Tintin'.

A Tintin was a cub reporter given that nickname by old hands on account of a disgusting fresh-faced keenness. There were quite a few at *The Post* in those days. Some of these went on to good careers on the nationals, or TV even. You'll know one or two of them, beneficiaries of some passing fad for more Northern voices in the media. You see them, babyfaces grown properly grizzled, popping up giving background on big political events. Elections, budgets, coup attempts, ministerial sackings, strikes. A lot of them have grown very pompous in their middle age.

Of the ones that didn't make it quite a few are dead or, worse, almost dead. The Last Golden Age of Regional Journalism was also the Last Golden Age of All-Day Liquid Lunch. A time when every interaction – with colleagues, with informants, with interviewees – was lubricated with hard liquor. Alcoholism was an occupational hazard. Relationships were cemented by drinking marathons and the fall-outs from them. The tragically inappropriate one-night stands, the undignified fist fights and the full English breakfasts eaten at 4pm. Cheap sausages as big a killer as the booze. The 1980s were also The Golden Age of the Chain Smoker and that didn't help the long-term health outcomes of a lot of my former colleagues.

A depressing number of my one-time peers and mentors have ended up hearing voices and shouting at shadows, monologuing at glassy-eyed strangers in out-of-the-way dives, bumming fags and trying to avoid looking at their yellowed and wasting skin in the mirror when they go to the gents. Which they do frequently. Pissing straight gets harder every year, while erections grow softer or disappear altogether. Some of these guys live in jittery dread of a knock on the door from the historical offence police too.

But these aren't even the most tragic casualties.

No, the saddest cases are the ones who fell victim to the insipid enticements of PR. I have seen some of the best minds of my generation end up as press officers for local authorities. Communications Directors for public utilities. Taking up jogging. Doing charity half-marathons. Filling up page after breathless page with their achievements on LinkedIn.

Anyway, no one ever wanted to be called a Tintin and

so I confided in him the reason for the dramatic change in my attitude.

'Oh, a *bird*!' he said, delighted. 'Why didn't you say?'

After I'd confessed, old Schatz helped my campaign where he could. Promoted me to Senior Reporter and he gave me the pick of the juicy stories. He got me to lead on some great *Post* campaigns – against tree felling in the city centre, for more nursery places, for naming and shaming able-bodied drivers who use disabled spaces in council car parks. I headed up campaigns demanding that the city get its proper share of central government funding for housing, health, education, sport and the arts. He fixed up some great interviews too – I got to talk to a twinkly Madonna, a saucy Tina Turner, a chatty Saul Bellow, a charming John Lydon, a difficult Tom Cruise. I even got five minutes with a thoughtful Muhammed Ali on his way to some memorabilia auction in Manchester. I have the photos of these encounters on the wall in Ernies.

Sometimes other reporters would complain about this blatant favouritism. Dear old Nick Schatz would just say: 'He's trying to punch above his weight with a lady. The poor lad needs all the help he can get.'

So I saw off the badminton player, as well as the other unseen and unknown rivals that must have been out there. I held my nerve too. Made no clumsy lunges, but also never pretended that I just wanted to be her friend, and eventually one Thursday, after the pubs were closed and we were giddy on a storming pub quiz victory, when my byline was on the front page (POST HELPS NAIL TOWPATH BEAST) and the back page (POST EXCLUSIVE: UNITED TO GET NEW OWNER) as well as the centre spread celebrity interview (U2 FRONTMAN BONO SHARES HIS PAIN WITH POST) Selena asked if I was going to get around to snogging her ever. Had that ever crossed my mind? I had to admit that it had. A few times actually.

'I'd go for it if I were you,' she said.

That was quite a good night.

Selena moved in by degrees. Clothes and make-up left around mine. There were things bought to cheer up my flat. Lamps and pictures. Cushions and rugs. A new kettle. Until finally, a row with her landlord about his inability to fix a leaky shower brought her to mine permanently.

She left uni that summer and started applying for jobs she was not quite qualified for and probably a bit too young for. It was a strategy that served her well over the years that followed. Included as a wild card on interview panels, her obvious energy, intelligence and refreshingly original tendency to say exactly what she thought would often get her the job. Her looks – lips, skin, teeth, etc. – they probably didn't hurt either, but she negotiated the inevitable workplace sexual harassment with some aplomb. With grace and eloquence.

'Try that again and I'll punch you in the fucking face,' she would say, pleasantly. Or words to that effect. Then she would start looking for another job that she wasn't quite qualified for, that she was just a bit too young for.

I never really knew quite what it was she was doing for these companies. If asked, she would just say that she was hired to shake things up, give some fresh insight, a bit of propulsion maybe. 'A kick up the corporate backside, that's what I deliver, Luke.'

In this way she made her way up the employment ladder until she was thirty-eight. By this time we were living in a big house in a nice area – all our neighbours were doctors and lawyers – and she was deciding that the time was right to have children. I hadn't thought about kids. Not really.

'It's lucky that I have then,' said Selena. 'I've been thinking for both of us.'

She told me she wanted two – a boy and a girl. They would be intelligent, they would be sporty and they would speak foreign languages and play musical instruments. More than this, they would be good and kind. They would use their talents to make the world a better place. It was our duty to have these kids.

'Okay,' I said. 'If you put it like that.'

There have been bumps in the child-rearing road. Of course there have. There always are. Illnesses, accidents, some friendship issues. A little light bullying perpetrated by Grace in Year 8, a spot of casual school refusing by Charlie in Year 9. The great Sports Day Crisis of 2006, the year Charlie didn't win anything. A decidedly difficult parents' evening in 2015 – the year it turned out Grace had told staff she was her mother's carer to excuse missing homework – but nothing we couldn't handle, nothing that couldn't be resolved with goodwill, time or cash. There was my redundancy to deal with of course, but even that turned out okay.

Selena's career had progressed with some velocity and now included being headhunted for directorships. Mine began to progress in the opposite direction. Not my fault, though I guess the high point of my career had been reached the night Selena had suggested we do some serious fooling around. My motivation slackened considerably after that, but it wasn't my main workplace difficulty.

No, the real problem at the *Post* was that people started migrating to the web to get their news, and the advertising revenue followed them. The people – those bastards – decided that paying for anything was an imposition. Particularly news. The masses seemed to think that twenty-first-century news should be free. Decided that if they had to pay for the real stuff, then they'd rather have the fake crap that didn't cost them anything.

Newspapers started shedding staff – especially trained and expensive staff – and so our content grew shoddier and more like the free crap peddled online anyway. Unsurprisingly, this did not quite arrest the drift away from print.

The idea of taking over Ernies grew from a piece of idle whimsy, a what-if-the-axe-really-does-fall conversation over a Sunday pub lunch. The initial idea was mine but everything else happened because Selena made it happen.

The morning after the night where we first talked about it I woke up with a hangover, while Selena woke up determined to see if the idea had legs. It became a project. It was Selena who kept an eye on the commercial property websites and when that axe really did fall it was Selena who offered up some of her savings to add to my redundancy payout so that I could buy the freehold of one of my favourite caffs.

'You better make a success of this, Luke,' she said. 'That's a big chunk of my fuck-off fund you've got there.'

The fuck-off fund. Right from when she had moved in with me Selena had insisted on the importance of every woman having a financial parachute. An escape route. A tunnel out.

I suppose by the time she left I'd got used to thinking of the fund as a kind of emergency thing for both of us, a cushion for when big-ticket items – cars, boilers, roofs, children – needed sorting out. I hadn't expected the fund to be used for actually fucking off.

I sat in Ernies until midnight. Maybe I should have gone home. Back to the old house. Back to the place that she'd fucked off from. But I couldn't do it. Home was just too big and empty and sad a place to be just then. It was while I was thinking this – thinking about the impossibility of moving from my chair in Paperwork Corner – that I remembered where I'd met the bloke I'd seen at the Hobbs house, the guy kicking off his shoes by the door. Remembered his name too. Micky Pitts. I knew then I couldn't do the catering for their bloody party. He had a lot more hair back when I was dealing with him. Was thinner too. But it was definitely him.

Which was a relief, frankly. It's always good to have a solidly moral reason for not going somewhere, for not doing something.

9

DOGS KNOW

A slow Tuesday. Breakfast done with, and I was taking the opportunity to grab a sausage buttie for myself when Wes and Zoe told me that they had decided to take me in hand.

'Enough is enough,' Zoe said.

I was puzzled at first. The remark seemed to come from nowhere and not relate to anything.

'What?' I said.

'You're getting to be a right lard-arse, mate,' said Wes.

'We're putting you on a *regime*,' said Zoe. She wrapped her tongue around the word with evident relish.

'You do know I'm actually the boss here, right?' I said. 'You know you're both meant to show me some respect?'

They looked at each other and smiled. I suppose I could've got mardy about it but I couldn't be arsed. Some places people would be fired for giving the boss this kind of lip. Other places – places not far from here – people would get a slap.

Anyway, it was true, I guess. I had been putting on the pounds. Piling them on actually. And no wonder. Since Selena left I'd been eating all the time. Eating badly too. Curries. Chow meins. Pizzas. Kebabs. Maybe it *was* getting out of hand. Even at work I seemed to have upgraded from an early morning toast and marmite to the closest we have to signature dish. Yeah, I was scoffing a full mega-breakfast most days.

I'd been eating my own weight in chocolate, too. The kind I used to spend my pocket money on as a kid. The ones that had the best adverts, or the best tunes anyway. *A finger of fudge is just enough to give your kids a treat . . . The Milkybar Kid is strong and tough . . .* I remember wanting to actually be the Milkybar Kid when I was young. Like lots of borderline dyspraxic no-good-at-football-or-fighting boys, I identified with him. Despite his weedy frame, his freckled face, his NHS specs, his crooked teeth, his generally punchable face, in the adverts the Milkybar Kid somehow got to be the leader of the gang. The Milkybar Kid gave us all hope.

Then there were the crisps. Not the good oven-baked kind either. I was munching down the worst kind, the maximum E-number kind. Your Wotsits, your Quavers, your Frazzles. Then there were the late-night crumpets and muffins. Cake. Cake at all hours, including before I headed off for work. Mr Kipling's finest. The fondant fancies. The lemon slices. The Bakewell tarts.

Then there was the booze thing. The doing no exercise thing. The lying awake worrying thing. Scaring myself with the rolling news in the early hours thing. All takes its toll.

'Thing is, bud, you look like shit,' said Wes.

'Proper shit,' said Zoe. 'And when did you last have a shower?'

I couldn't remember. But it was only a few days before. I just don't like being wet first thing in the morning. Anyway, I was waking in skin that felt borrowed, felt like it didn't fit. My skin was not my skin, so it hardly mattered if it was clean or not.

'Thanks for the support, gang,' I said.

'This *is* support,' said Zoe. 'We're not standing by and watch you neglect yourself to death. There's nothing more supportive than that. We're saving you from yourself.'

'Staging an intervention,' said Wes. Then he said – and said it as if it was a profound existentialist insight, like he was frigging Nietzsche in a sodding pinny: 'You can't mend a broken heart with food.'

'I'm not a love-sick teenager,' I said. 'I'm not a kid moping in his bedroom because his crush has snogged someone else at the disco.'

'No,' said Zoe. 'No, you're not.'

'Right,' I said.

'It would be better if you were,' she said. 'That would be okay. You'd have an excuse to behave like this then. Teenagers moping over the death of their first love, they get a pass. You don't. You have to . . .' She paused to search for the right phrase.

'You have to man up,' said Wes.

'Well, I wouldn't—' said Zoe.

'Show some balls,' said Wes. 'Grow some fucking cojones.'

Zoe rolled her eyes. There was a silence.

'Okay,' I said. 'So what's the plan? What is this famous regime?'

It turned out that they did have something worked out. Which meant they'd been talking it over, thinking hard about it. Genuinely working together to try and pull me out of the pit they saw I'd got myself into. This slough of despond. A slough – whatever that is – filled with fats and sugars. Bad carbs. It made me a bit teary, the idea that there were people looking out for me, wanting to help. This was the other thing that had been happening since Selena left: every time I saw someone being nice to someone else I'd been welling up.

Someone getting a takeout bacon sarnie for a homeless guy. Someone soothing someone else's kid when the kid is frantic and the mother at her wits' end. Someone buying an early morning brew for a shivering working girl. These are the kindnesses I saw every day in Ernies and they took me to the very edge of tears every single time. I was getting so I couldn't be trusted at the till, always under-charging and letting people off. Zoe had to have a word more than once. Said that it'd alert the taxman if we weren't careful.

When I watched movies at home I was even worse. Even more of a wreck. The kindnesses are bigger in the films, I guess. In a movie whole lives are put back together in the final scenes. Children and animals are saved from disaster. Love begins and blossoms and heads to the altar. Songs are sung. Orchestral music swells. People kiss.

Plus, in the films the people giving or receiving the favours were more beautiful than was generally the case in Ernies. Exposure to all that beauty damages the psyche.

Yes, I got soppy and sentimental since my wife left me. Bite me.

'Let's go upstairs,' said Zoe.

Upstairs at Ernies was a flat originally. When Selena and I bought the freehold we thought we'd do the place up, rent it out. Which would also mean we'd have someone living on-site the whole time, which would be good for the security of the place. But you know how it is, it needed a lot of work and we just never got around to it. For a while we tried using it as a kind of staff restroom. I put an old three-piece suite up there: a kettle, a fridge and a microwave. But, you know, why traipse upstairs to what's essentially a cheerless bedsit for a brew and a sit-down when there's a proper functioning café down-stairs? Especially when said café was empty of customers a lot of the time and so felt like a personal chill-out space anyway.

Pretty soon the flat became a damp depository for junk – broken chairs and tables that we might one day get around to fixing or taking to the dump.

It had been transformed now. It was a proper – if bijou – gym. The broken chairs had gone. It had been nuked clean too, the air bright with the same lemon and vinegar combo that defined the kitchen. The floors were swept and hoovered. The sofa was in the bedroom, and where it used to squat there was now a heavy boxing bag. Weights of various sizes were in neat sets in one corner of the room. There were skipping ropes, gloves and pads in the others.

'Boxercise,' I said. 'Seriously?'

'I'm sorry, would you rather do Zumba? A spin class? Step-fucking-aerobics?' Zoe was irritated. There was a beat and then her voice softened. 'It really works, Luke. Look at me.' She stepped back, adopted a pugilist's crouch and shadow-boxed, throwing combinations of punches, making all the noises as she did it. *Puh puh pu-puh puh*. She did a little Ali shuffle. Even in her apron she somehow looked the part.

'Big history of boxing in Hungary,' said Wes. 'Especially in the lighter divisions.'

I looked at Zoe more closely. Perhaps she was more toned than she had been. More definition to her cheekbones maybe. More breadth to the shoulders. A brighter glow to her skin. She stopped punching her invisible opponent, ran her hand through her hair, tossed it theatrically. Pouted in mock annoyance. 'Honestly, Luke. I'm proper hot these days. I'm a sex goddess and you haven't even noticed. You've grown dead to beauty, my friend, no wonder . . .'

She stopped there. The rest of the sentence reverberated despite not being voiced. *No wonder your wife left you.*

'No offence,' she said. She had the grace to look embarrassed.

'It's not boxercise anyway. We're going to do proper boxing training,' said Wes. 'It's a waste of time otherwise.'

Zoe jumped in to tell me that boxing was Wes's thing. The other thing he learned in prison along with the cheffing. Now he was going to do bags and pads with me when we were quiet. Meanwhile her role would be to draw up a nutrition plan and make sure I stick to it. She was going to monitor my progress and decide on appropriate rewards when I hit my weekly targets.

'If you want to lose weight ask a recovering anorexic,' she said. 'We know all the tricks.'

It was the first time she'd mentioned having been anorexic, though I had often wondered, like I'd wondered about the scars you could just make out beneath the tattoos on her arms.

She said she'd got me something to help me stay motivated in the exercise department. A sort of analogue fitbit.

'I'm not wearing any devices,' I said.

Zoe snorted. 'You're not listening properly. Analogue, I said.' She headed back downstairs while Wes gave me my first lesson – how to wrap my hands properly, how to stand, how to snap out a jab, always making sure I get my hand coming back to my face. He seemed impressed. Or he feigned being impressed pretty well.

'Fast hands.' He sounded genuinely surprised. 'You'll be okay.'

I felt an absurdly powerful rush of gratitude. I almost hugged him. I welled up. Got away with it. Didn't start crying properly. Blew my nose.

'Thanks,' I said.

* * *

73

That analogue fitbit? Turned out to be a dog.

Zoe popped out while I was punching the pads with Wes and came back with a sad-eyed Alsatian.

'Meet your new best friend,' she said.

'You are joking,' I said.

I'd never had a dog before. We had no pets growing up and neither did my own kids. Selena and I were so busy we never felt we'd have the time to look after them properly and the kids never seemed too keen anyway. Whenever they mooted the idea of a pet they were easily bought off with games or bikes or phones. I've always been a bit scared of dogs, to be honest. If my life had ever depended on my having a pet, I'd have got a tortoise or a fish. Something quiet and low-maintenance. Certainly not something whose shit you had to pick up and carry around in your pockets like a squidgy hand-warmer. Not something where you had to fork out a fortune to have it looked after when you went away. Not something with teeth.

The few times we talked about it, Selena and I were agreed. Dogs are like kids who never grow up. Any unconditional love you might get from them is well out-weighed by the expense and the inconvenience. Then they just get sick and die on you. A dying dog costs a bloody fortune too.

And all that futile noise. The excited – but mono-tonous – yapping that is just a way of announcing that they have seen something. *What's that you say, Fido? What? You've spotted another dog? That's truly amazing! How wonderful! You deserve all the treats today, you clever old thing, you.*

Not for me.

Anyway, as an old journo I cared about the welfare of all the kids who delivered newspapers. Every dog sees himself as a member of an elite royal protection squad.

Even the most slovenly mongrel terrier imagines himself as an SAS guardian of the backyard. Every time they go after a kid with a sack it's like they're foiling a fatwa.

I was pretty sure that my opinion on dogs was that they were noisy, dirty and thick. Only turned out I was wrong. Turned out I didn't think that. Not really. No, instead of rejecting her the way I thought I would, I fell in love with her immediately. Though I didn't let myself show it. Not at first.

'Having a dog will help keep you trim,' Zoe said. 'All that walking. And she'll stop you getting socially isolated too. Dog owners are a friendly bunch. Always up for a chat.'

This was actually another reason I had never wanted a dog. The fact that you'd have to have conversations with other dog owners as you did your twice daily trudge around the neighbourhood, or wandered in the park chucking a saliva-soaked tennis ball trying to figure out which of the other men there was a flasher. I'd always been of the opinion that if you wanted a dog to keep you fit then why didn't you get an imaginary one? You could decide on the breed in your head – make it a really bloody active one if you wanted – and just set off twice a day for the required time with no need to stick plastic bags of faeces in your pockets.

'Where is she from?' I said.

Zoe was airy and vague: 'Oh, a mate is having to move and the new landlord won't take pets. But look, do you really not want her? I thought you'd be pleased actually. I thought you liked dogs. You let people bring them in here.'

'They are paying for the privilege,' I said. But then I couldn't see the point in arguing any more. I should just give in now. This was the sort of thing that always annoyed Selena, the way I'd argue over things that didn't really matter. The way I'd take a stand over things I didn't even believe in.

'What's her name?'

'Juliet,' she said.

'Not as in Romeo though, as in Bravo,' said Wes.

'What?'

'Ex-police dog,' he said.

I remembered now, *Juliet Bravo* was the first British cop show to feature a female lead. It was a decent show. No Z-cars but pretty good anyway. My mum loved it.

'You know, Luke, being responsible for the welfare of another living creature is good for the soul. Stops you becoming too self-absorbed. Keeps you connected to the world. Keeps you grounded. You do know this, right? And Juliet is such a sweet thing. Soft as butter.'

Regardless of the fact that I did actually like the bloody dog, I wanted to ask her what was so good about being connected to the world? Who wants to be kept grounded? Being grounded didn't just mean down to earth after all, it was also a punishment, right? It's what you did to kids who had misbehaved. But I didn't ask this because I was distracted by the fact Selena had come into the café. And she wasn't on her own. She was with a young bloke. An absurdly young bloke. An absurdly good-looking young bloke. Looked like he should be in the movies. Action flicks. A superhero just before he realises he has special powers that he can use to save humanity from itself. He had that kind of soulful intensity. Jacob.

Juliet bared her teeth and growled. She broke into furious barks. Zoe had to hold her back to stop her lunging at the intruders. She didn't seem all that sweet and not at all butter-like now. It was an impressively scary performance. This dog was clearly a great judge of character.

'Of course I'll take her,' I said. 'I can tell already that we're going to be pals.'

10

THE BIGGER PERSON

We sat around a table at the window. This Jacob had the bold fucking front to order our mega-breakfast, our gut-buster. Double eggs, double bacon, double sausage with black pudding and hash browns and beans and everything. I was hoping he would choke on it and I also hoped he knew that he was paying full price for it. He asked for it to come with a Coke rather than tea or coffee. Explained that he had never got on with hot drinks.

I looked at Selena as he said this. I projected my thoughts towards her. Your lover is an actual child, my thoughts said. He doesn't belong in the world of adults, the realm of real men and real women.

It was if she'd heard me. She raised her eyes and they met mine briefly. I was unmoored by the warm honey of them, the brown heat of them. She grimaced and her eyes flickered away. There was a twisting in my guts.

Jacob was looking around too and I found myself seeing the café through his eyes. The mismatched chairs. The scarred tables. The faded photos of my encounters from the *Post* days. The plastic sauce bottles. The regulars: Sad Rosie and her wordsearch book and her absent stare; the two Jennies tapping at their phones while their piglet-fat baby Eddard played with a tablet in the buggy, stabbed at it with chipolata fingers; Ken and his toast;

Old Chas Diggle with his receding green Mohawk, sixty years old and the last punk in town; Juliet, who, exhausted by her vigorous denunciation of my wife's lover, had gone to sleep in Paperwork Corner.

Fuck you, Jacob, I thought. Don't you come in here judging me and my clientele. Tallying up my achievements and finding them wanting. Don't you dare do that.

I knew already that Jacob wasn't from around here. He wasn't even from the North. His voice had the manicured tone they give you in southern private schools. It was a voice that had compulsory prep and fives and choir practice embedded in it. Selena used to hate RP too. Said it set her teeth on edge. Made her want to plant bombs at the last night of the proms.

'Nice place,' he said in the end. 'Very clean.'

Patronising wanker. Of course it was clean. It was also the heart and fucking soul of the community. I should have given him a slap and then I should have thrown him out right then. Instead I just asked him if he wanted fried bread or toast.

'Fried bread!' he chirped, clapping his hands together. 'Haven't had that since I was a kid. I presume it'll be cooked in lard?'

Oh, my word. You *presume*, do you? Well, you presume wrong, old bean. No, it won't be cooked in lard, you twonk. It's not 1953. Who uses lard? You'll have it cooked in rice bran oil like everyone else.

Zoe passed by on her way to give Ken more toast. She put her free hand on my shoulder. This small gesture of solidarity nearly undid me completely. I felt the tears coming. I excused myself and heard how choked and tight my voice had become.

In the kitchen Zoe asked if I wanted to enhance Jacob's dining experience. Gob in the mushrooms. Nose pickings sprinkled like truffle shavings on the eggs. Or worse. I remember a story she told once of working in a place where the chef was known to toss off into the food if a customer pissed him off.

Wes wasn't keen. He had his reputation to think of, and I found myself backing him up. This Jacob might have nicked my wife, but you've got to rise above it, haven't you? Have to be the bigger man. Person. In the end.

'I have never been the bigger person,' Zoe said. She seemed genuinely puzzled about why anyone would want to be. 'People mess with me or those I love then they get fucked up. End of and simple as.'

Sometimes you could really see why the medieval era appealed to her.

I tried to remind her that she was the one who said my wife leaving was completely normal and was part of a global trend, actually. Just the way of the modern world.

'So I contradict myself? So what? Anyway, I just don't like this Jacob bloke. I don't like his face.'

'What's wrong with his face?' said Wes.

'It's too beautiful for a start,' she said. 'Take it from me, have nothing to do with a beautiful man. Don't trust them. They've had things way too easy and it's ruined them. I like my men a bit battered by life. I like them unbeautiful. Tragically, I also seem to like them skint.'

'Just as well,' said Wes.

Zoe did something surprising then. She gave Wes a long kiss full on the lips before hurrying back out into the cafe.

I looked at Wes. He shrugged.

'We were going to tell you,' he said.

Which is how I learned that Zoe and Wes were an item, or having a bit of a thing at the very least. It's how I learned that Juliet had been Wes's dog but now that he was moving in with Zoe he needed to find a good new home for her. Zoe's landlord was the one that wouldn't allow pets. The fact that Wes and Zoe were together was another thing that made me feel a bit weepy. The knowledge that they chose me as foster dad for their pet, that made me fill up too.

I really did need to get a grip.

Back at the table we did tense chit-chat for a while. Polite enough. Jacob murmured condescending appreciation of his breakfast. Splendid, tremendous, perfect, how did we get the bacon just the right amount of crisp? Yeah, yeah. The surprise in his voice was the most irritating thing. Why shouldn't we do the best crispy bacon in town?

Selena thanked me for my help in talking sense into the kids. I was a bit conflicted about this. It was true that I had been urging Charlie and Grace to get in touch with their mum, to be a bit kind to her, to show her some empathy. Encouraging them to see her adventure as a kind of breakdown, I guess. I'd been kind of implying that it would be all right, that she'd get this out of her system and things would return to a kind of normality. None of this was true but it was what they wanted to hear, I think. At the same time, I had been comforted by how angry they'd been with her. How they had taken my side.

I decided that I'd go and visit them soon. Maybe watch Charlie play rugby, maybe take Grace shopping. Have dinner with them both. Spoil them. Restore my advantage as Top Parent. Not very noble, I admit. Wasn't really playing the be-the-bigger-person game. But maybe Zoe's right, maybe it's a stupid game.

Eventually they got around to why they were here, in my café, ruining my day. Selena said that she was sorry to barge in on me like this. 'But you've become as slippery as an eel. Very hard to pin down.'

'We want to talk about moving things forward.' This was Jacob.

'*Practicalities*,' I said, stressing the word.

He didn't seem to notice the steel in my tone. Or if he did, he ignored it.

'Practicalities, that's right. We're under a bit of time pressure. Thing is . . .' He took a breath. 'Thing is, we actually want take a bit of time off, don't we, darling? Go travelling or something. And it'd be nice to have things sorted by then.'

He was such a child that his voice did that teenage rising inflection thing, as though he was asking a question. Asking permission. And *darling*? He was *darling* her now?

I looked at Selena. God, she looked tired. The electricity in her face was dimmed somehow. She didn't look my way, but she knew I was studying her. I could tell by her sad smile. By the way she pulled at her hair.

'You're going to take a gap year?' I said.

She turned to me. Looked me straight in the eye. I was unmoored. So beautiful. I gripped the edge of the table.

'Yeah, why not? I've been working for thirty-odd years, and when I've not been working I've generally been sorting stuff out at home. That's been like a whole other job.'

'What stuff?'

'Shopping, cooking, cleaning, the holidays, the direct debits, the MOT for the car, the fucking play dates, who is doing what and where and working out how they're getting there. The PTA. And fucking Christmas. All the fucking Christmases. That stuff. Yes, I know you've done what you can. But I'm sick of it, Luke. I could do with a proper break.'

Jacob got very animated too. He was practically bouncing up and down in his seat. He liked my analogy. 'Yeah, a gap year. That's it exactly. We want some proper adventures together, make some memories. A gap year. I like that.' Which was annoying.

'This will actually be your second gap year, won't it?' I realised straight away that this was the wrong approach. I'd made it seem like the main reason I was critical of him was that he was getting more than his fair share of hiking time. Made it look like I was pissed off with him for frivolously wasting his time tweeting from Angkor Wat or taking selfies at Ayers Rock or Machu fucking Picchu or wherever, rather than because he'd stolen my wife.

'Ours might actually be more than a year. In the end,' said Selena. 'I said a proper break and I bloody mean it.'

'We quite fancy having a gap life, don't we, love?' This was Jacob. He sniggered like he'd said something very witty.

I was scalded by his casual use of the words *we* and *love*, scalded too by seeing her reach across to take his hand. I think the sudden pain of this made me a bit stupid because it took me a while to work out exactly what she was talking about. I got there in the end.

'You want to sell the house?'

Selena looked away again. 'It's fair enough, Luke. It'll be good for you too, you know. A fresh start in your own place,' she said.

'The kids won't like it,' I said.

'That again. Look, the kids have gone, Luke. They're on their own now, pretty much. Plus they're coming round to the new situation. We always said we'd sell up when they were off our hands.'

Yes, I thought. *We* were going to sell up. *We* were going to go travelling. Maybe get a vintage camper van. Go to the States. Drive Route 66 and Highway 61. We were going have a gap year of our own. Not that we called it that. That was *our* plan, Selena, I wanted to say, mine and yours. Not yours and this molly-coddled, baby-faced prick's.

82

'I need a piss,' I said. I stood up.

Jacob mumbled something. I didn't catch what he said. He nudged Selena.

'Oh, yeah, Luke, there's something else.' She took a breath, visibly braced herself. 'I want to sell my share in the café too.'

There was a silence. There was so much to say here. Where to start?

'Right,' I said.

'We can talk about it more later. Sort out whether we sell it altogether or whether you buy me out. You don't have to decide right this second.'

She couldn't look at me while she said it and I thought later that this was the only time I'd ever known Selena behave in a cowardly way. But while she was here in the room, actually saying this stuff to me I couldn't think at all, let alone respond as I should.

'Right,' I said again.

'Really was an amazing breakfast,' said Jacob.

'Thanks,' I said, stupidly.

Then, thank God, Zoe was at my side.

'Everyone finished?' she said, breezy as you like. 'Good. Two coffees and a full English. That'll be £11.95 then, thank you.'

There was a pause. Selena and Jacob looked at me. Clearly I was meant to let them off the bill. Well, fuck that.

Selena sighed and Jacob said not to worry he'd get it. I clocked the way his eyes wandered all over Zoe. I wondered if Selena saw it too. A good sign for me, I thought.

'I really do need a piss,' I said.

11

A PRIVATE WORD

The bog in Ernies is small. Just one urinal, a stall and a tiny sink. Everything squashed too close together to be properly comfortable. I needed a few minutes to sit down and think. I got the sitting down part done, but thinking was harder. Coherent thoughts were blocked by the surging of a murderous rage.

When I came out there was Jacob waiting by the door. Filling the space. All shoulders.

'I wanted a private word,' he said. 'Just me and you. Clear the air a bit.'

Outside in the café proper, the muffled sound of everyday chit-chat. The radio. A distant drilling. Jacob carried on, 'I wanted to say that I do love Selena, you know. I'll treat her properly. Take care of her and everything.'

Everything? And *everything*? What did that even mean?

'Maybe we'll get married. I know Selena is too old for us to have children of our own but we've talked about adopting. Give a deprived kid a chance, you know.'

Which is when I snapped.

I took out that little vegetable knife I always have in my pocket – a wise precaution around here – and I stuck him. Thrust the knife in as far as I could, so far that I could feel the blade snag on a rib. I twisted my wrist as I hoiked it out. I was going to do all the damage I could.

He didn't scream, just sort of gasped. I plunged the blade back in again and again and again. I gouged him maybe twenty-five times. Going in as hard as I could every time. My hand always following the knife with a corkscrew motion. My arm ached with the effort of it. I was after the big arteries, the important targets. Chest. Neck. Thighs. Stomach. It wasn't just about Selena. There was other stuff going on, I admit it. That's for the film star grin, the Hollywood teeth. That's for being six foot two. That's for the artfully mussed hair. That's for the stubble. For the broad shoulders. The long legs. That's for the drawing room vowels and the easy privilege. That's for being twenty-six. That's for presuming. That's for all of it. Oh, look, seems even the beautiful bleed and gasp and gurgle and beg for their lives.

There was blood everywhere. Jets of it. All over him, all over me, painting the walls and floor of the restroom. So much of it. Who knew people contained so much blood? So vivid. So bright. And the last thing I did before bracing myself to go out and tell Selena that the gap year thing was probably not going to happen now, was to slash Jacob's stupidly pretty face from his ear to his mouth and the same on the other side. Cut him a clown mouth in good old Stonebeck style. No way was I letting him leave a good-looking corpse.

I know. I didn't do that. Any of it. You know it. It crossed my mind, though. I could have done it. I could have got away with it too. Claimed he went for me first. Self-defence. *Didn't know I had a knife in my hand, Officer. Was just trying to protect myself.* Fact, I could say it was his knife. I took it off him, or turned his hand as I was avoiding his first blow. I'm actually the victim here, Your Honour. This Jacob kid came armed and ready to do me damage. Malice aforethought.

But, no.

Instead – in real life – I just told him that I thought he was a bit of a knob and watched his face go purple. I thought he was going to hit me. I braced myself. I had time to wonder if I'd hit back. By then I was so all over the place emotionally that I had no idea what my own reactions to anything were likely to be. I was like a puppet, like there was someone else with their hand up my jacksie deciding how I responded to things. A ventriloquist doing my thinking and speaking for me and doing it badly.

Anyway, I think my wife's lover might have throttled me had someone not tried to open the door behind him. He sighed and shuffled over to make room for the door to open fully. He muttered an apology. Very polite. Well mannered. That's southern private schools for you. That's what the parents are paying for. Along with getting the Oxbridge places, the decent jobs and keeping the kids from being despoiled by contact with the lower orders, it's nice to think that your children will also be taught to say please and thank you.

The bloke squeezing in? It was Ken. Bless him.

'Room for a little'un?' Ken said.

12

SILLY MONEY

The old guy in the good suit had a small veggie breakfast, and he apologised for it. Said that back in the day he
could have finished a gut-buster without thinking about
it. This happens surprisingly often in the modern café,
older men getting mournful about their declining capac-
ity to put away the meat and carbs the way they once did.
Zoe's theory was that they saw a dwindling of the appe-
tite as another sign that death was lurking somewhere
nearby, sharpening his scythe. Ironing his shroud.
Hovering at their table like a waiter with the chip-and-
pin machine, waiting to whisper that it's time to get on
home, Daddy's waiting.

She also says that in apologising for going for a lighter
bite these men are also saying sorry for the way that
they've let life make them fearful, timid. The way it has
unmanned them. She says that of course they're also
apologising in advance for impotence.

'Like any of us care,' she says. 'Like they're ever going
to get the chance for it to matter.'

This bloke was a mild-looking sort. Pretty anony-
mous. Not thin, not fat. His hair scanty and mouse-grey.
At first glance he was just a standard old geezer. Look
closely though and you could see there was an ego there.
The suit was well-cut in dark cloth. It could even have

been a Michelsberg or a Hemingway. He wore one of those watches they advertise on the back of the glossier mens' mags. You know the ones – you never own a something-or-other watch, you just look after it for future generations. That bollocks. The truth is that however fancy, however highly machined, this watch will get lost or broken just like everything else does. In this case it was too chunky for his skinny wrist, so it was an heirloom that might disappear well before future generations got their paws on it.

Still, despite the suit, despite the watch, and despite the well-maintained teeth, despite the almost regimental-ish tie, despite the Loake brogues, and the jaunty socks, he still managed to look like a bingo caller with delusions of grandeur. Or the doorman of some hotel that had seen better days. Much better days. The clothes were wearing him somehow.

When he asked me to sit down with him for a bit of a chinwag, I did it because I felt a bit sorry for him. Because I thought he was just another lonely widower looking for human contact and for a way to fill the long, long days. We get quite a few of those in Ernies.

He introduced himself as Tony. 'I used to love coming here,' he said. 'Was a real sanctuary for me back in the day. A home from home. Looks like it still is for some people.'

He nodded towards where Sad Rosie sat, day-dreaming over her daily cuppa.

I didn't say anything. My plan was to just let the old guy talk. Let him reminisce if he wanted, I had time. At this point I still thought I was doing him a favour. Providing him with some vital human contact in the desert of another day.

'I knew the original owner,' he said now. 'Darius Peretsky.'

'Original owner was an Earnshaw surely?' I said.

He smiled. 'No, Darius called it Earnshaws because he wanted a name that sounded authentically Yorkshire. He'd been stationed here as a pilot during the war and fallen in love with the place. He wanted to serve the grub he'd learned to like but didn't think the locals would cope with getting their butties in a place called Peretsky's. I think he was wrong, as it happens. I think Yorkshire folk are more broad-minded than people give them credit for.'

This was a thing I'd often thought about. Not that us Yorkshire folk are broad-minded – that's contentious, to say the least – but I agree that the whole notion of authenticity is such bullshit. Built on very shaky foundations. Lots of the best things are inauthentic. Red pesto, for example. Chicken Madras. Rock and roll. I liked the idea that Ernies, a place apparently so quintessentially West Yorks was founded and built by a foreigner. It made me smile.

Zoe brought the food, looked at me curiously as she put the plate down.

'Party was good,' the guy said now, as he fastidiously spread a paper napkin over his bespoke trousers. 'You should have done it. We had venison burgers from a guy from out Harrogate way in the end. It was pretty decent. Can't beat a decent fry-up though.'

It was only then that I realised who I was talking to.

'Tony Hobbs,' I said.

He smiled for long enough that I could see that these were really very expensive teeth. 'The very same.'

Just as he owned up to this Micky Pitts arrived, flustered, all apologies. As he sat down, he provided a list of excuses. There was traffic. Joanie couldn't find her keys. The dogs needed to be walked. You know how it is. Hobbs said nothing but his posture radiated weary disdain. I got the feeling that Micky Pitts was often all apologies, often offering excuses, often saying that you know how it is. An impression that was reinforced when Hobbs turned to me and told me that he knew the real reason we hadn't taken the catering gig at his recent party.

'It was because of Micky here, wasn't it? You caught a glimpse of his face on your way out of my house and decided then and there to blow me out.'

It was true, I guess. When I'd finally processed that the bloke I'd seen getting his wellies off in the Hobbs's hallway was same skid mark that we had exposed in *The Post* twenty years ago, I'd known I couldn't work for his employer. Though if Wes and Zoe had shown even a hint of enthusiasm we might have done it anyway.

'Micky has been messing things up for years,' Hobbs said now. 'He's a liability. But he's the daughter's husband.' He spread his hands as if to say what can you do?

Yes. What can you do about Micky Pitts and people like him? It's a good question but one I could have answered once upon a time.

Micky Pitts had been a bouncer back in the eighties, one who used his position as a doorman at various clubs to deal nasty drugs to nice kids. Badly cut ketamine was his speciality. There are several once-promising students, solicitors now or teachers, who can never be more than a hundred yards from a public toilet because of the Special K that Micky sold them. One or two ended up in an even worse state, handsome once-sporty boys wearing adult nappies while still in their twenties.

Police wouldn't do much about Micky so *The Post* went after him. I went after him. Bad luck for Micky that the pinnacle of his drug supply career coincided with the peak of my efforts to impress Selena.

I was like a dog with a bone. Wouldn't let it lie. And I got him on the front page eventually, head inefficiently covered with a blanket in the photo. But we employed a great court artist in those days. Caught his likeness to an absolute tee.

Pitts got ten years in 1989, but everyone knew we'd only nailed a foot soldier. Micky never said who the real boss was. He might have been stupid but he wasn't suicidal. I was thinking about all this – going through the cuttings library of my mind – when Micky spoke.

'No hard feelings by the way,' he said, looking straight at me. 'I learned a lot inside.'

'Yeah, and almost none of it useful,' said his father-in-law. 'Micky got himself a few GCSEs, even an –ology or two but still, if it wasn't for Joanie I don't think he'd have a job. Certainly not with me. Micky's just one of those people. A fuck-up. It's not his fault. He just is.'

Micky laughed. 'It's true. I'm just one of those people.'

With that he summoned Zoe over and ordered a full English – a gut-buster with a third egg and chips on the side. Tony Hobbs closed his eyes for a long second. This evidence of someone else's continuing desire for things he'd had to leave behind himself causing him real grief. I knew how he felt. I wasn't there yet but I knew one day I would be and that knowledge was painful enough.

I said nowt. Moments passed. The clink of cutlery. The sound of chit and chat from the customers. Did you watch that thing last night? Channel Four? Yeah, mate, I was in bits.

The stereo played. Zoe's choice. Singer-songwriter type. Minor key. I couldn't make out the exact words but I could guess them: I loved him/ He didn't love me back/ He did some upsetting shit/ But, hey, fuck him/ His loss/ He's a wanker and I'm stronger now.

Something like that.

'Anyway, you're probably wondering why I'm here,' Hobbs said.

* * *

91

Tony Hobbs wanted to buy Ernies. Wanted to swallow the whole area in fact. He could see the opportunities offered by Stonebeck moving up in the world. A planned high-speed rail link was going to mean a new station, new commuter rabbit hutches, new bars and gyms. Craft grog shops and artisan bakeries. Shiny gated community fun for everyone.

Maybe a literary festival. Everyone else has got one, so why can't we?

Hobbs presented his involvement as a kind of philanthropy. He was going to be part of the solution to the age-old problems of the place. About time someone took a lead. The prostitutes and their scumbag punters would go for a start. He looked around. I followed his gaze. Yes, we had a couple of working girls in and yes, a couple of sad-faced men who might sometimes take their comfort there. I liked the sex workers actually. We all did. It's a tough life and they managed it better than you or I would. A hooker could always get a free hot drink at Ernies if she needed one. It was the least we could do.

'Nations are dead,' Hobbs said. 'Look across the world, countries have ripped themselves apart – but cities are thriving.'

Hobbs told me how he'd already got the council squared away and several other major partners on board. London firms. Global capital. Russians. Chinese. Americans. Brazilians. The architect he had in mind was Israeli. Had just designed a whole new city over there. Would have won international awards if it hadn't been built on occupied territory.

'Exciting times, Lukey, my man,' Micky said.

Yes, Hobbs continued. Yes, of course he hoped to make a few quid, but that wasn't the main reason he was doing it. 'I want to leave a legacy. To know I've done some good in the world with whatever remaining time I'm lucky enough to be granted.'

There followed a digression about how the old style Victorian philanthropists used to leave generous bequests: schools, churches, libraries, almshouses, arboretums. Hobbs said he'd been inspired by how the great industrialists of the past transformed the city in their day. How they built a real Northern powerhouse.

'Yeah, well,' I said. 'They were all religious, weren't they? Methodists and Baptists. Shitting themselves about going to hell if they couldn't present the Big Man with solid evidence of Good Deeds.'

'This is true. A belief in Satan is very useful when it comes to social progress,' he said. And that's right, I think. Billionaires these days are all atheists and can barely be bothered to contribute so much as a brick towards a new hospice and even that they write off against tax.

There was a pause while we reflected on the mean-spiritedness of the contemporary billionaire. The spiritual bankruptcy of the modern rich fucker.

It was into this pause that Micky Pitts's breakfast was delivered.

'Any condiments, sir?' Zoe said, her tone exaggeratedly respectful as if playing the maid in some am-dram drawing room comedy. She did this sort of thing occasionally, anything to keep herself entertained during a long shift.

Pitts laughed. He adopted a highfalutin Middle England voice. A BBC voice. A Jacob voice. 'A small dish of brown sauce would be most welcome, my dear,' he said.

My skin itched. After she'd gone, he grinned at me. 'I have to say, Luke, breakfast looks all right. Bit of a surprise after seeing the shitty reviews.'

Oh, right. I got it now. All those spiteful one-stars. Part of an air-war. A softening up process. Cyberbullying. I should have known; it occurred to me just then that at some level I *had* known.

When Hobbs spoke again it was to say that he was sure that I wouldn't want to hold back progress. Oh, and he would pay proper money of course, the market value and then some. It was a pretty good speech but I knew the damage he and his kind did on a daily basis. The hookers he wanted to get rid of wouldn't have to be hookers if it wasn't for him and people like him. Then there was Micky and the whole *Lukey, my man* thing. How could I let that go?

He told me that he'd already had my gaff looked over by a crack squad of architects and surveyors.

'The blokes who came in while I was up in Easeby meeting your wife,' I said.

'Exactly so. That was the main point of getting you up there, so I could get my team in to your place, give it the once-over. Assess potential. They say it's in pretty good nick. So, you know, hats off.'

I made a note to make sure Ken's next round of toast was on the house. I owed him an apology. He'd been very offended when I'd suggested he'd grassed us up to the council. Hadn't come in for a full three days. Zoe had had to go round his house to see if he was all right. Got sent away with a flea in her ear, but he'd started coming back in after that. He'd made his point, I guess.

Hobbs finally did the big reveal. Told me what he was willing to shell out to get hold of the café. Silly money. I remembered what his missus had said about not feeling he was getting the best unless he paid too much, but still I had to make him repeat it, just to be sure I'd heard right.

I had. Selena would be pleased. Would mean the fuck-off fund had made a very tidy return on its investment. Very tidy indeed. I should definitely think about it.

I didn't think about it. 'No, thank you,' I said.

He kept his face impassive, though his eyes flashed. He gestured for me to lean forward. I did and he whispered another number into my ear. It was exactly double that first insane figure. I was thinking, I should take it. I should definitely take it. Give Selena her share, pay off the kids' student loans, then have a holiday. The mother of all gap years. That's definitely what I should do.

I leaned forward a bit more. Tony leaned forward too. There was a stiffness there. The man needed to think about gentle stretching. Some kind of seniors' yoga class, aquarobics maybe. My lips were practically touching the fleshy ear lobe. I had a good view of his surprisingly dark ear hair.

My intention had been to tell him exactly where to go and to do it very forcefully, but when it came to it, it seemed somehow wrong to use any vulgarity. Instead I just growled out each bald syllable, tried to give each one the force of the crudest profanity. The fiercest eff and jeff. 'No. Thank. You.'

Hobbs jerked back from me, his face darkened, there was that flash in the eyes again. I thought he was going to bang the table. Jab his finger in my face. This was definitely a man used to getting his own way. He made a visible effort to get control of himself. Took an ostentatious Deep Breath.

'I get this,' he said. 'There's a lot of years invested here. A lot of your life. But sentiment is a luxury in business, I find. A costly one. In any case we can easily get a Compulsory Purchase Order and you'll find the council will be considerably less generous than me. They have the taxpayers to worry about, you see, have to be seen to be responsible with their cash.'

He pushed his plate away from him. His lackey did the same, though he had only just made a start on his breakfast and he spilled tomato juice onto the table. If you're a fuck-up, you're a fuck-up in everything. Your nature is revealed in the small acts as well as the big ones.

Hobbs took a last sip at his tea. Micky did the same. They stood to go. Hobbs made a very deliberate thing of shaking my hand. Micky just eyeballed me intently. A hard stare that was meant to be very Kray-twin but just came across as sub-Paddington. It's the kind of Poundland mobster thing you see all the time in Stonebeck. Boys and men puffing out their chests, giving their peers the evils, trying to come the hard man. It almost made me laugh.

'I'll say cheerio, then,' Hobbs said. He paused as if something important had just occurred to him. It was all very obvious, asking your question on the way out like it was an afterthought. Like a killer question had just struck you. In journalism we called it the Columbo move after the scruffy cop in the TV show. He was always doing it.

'Oh, you do know about your cook, don't you?'

'Wes?' I said.

'Yes, Wes. You know what he was put away for, don't you?'

'Of course,' I said. Which was a lie and I don't know why I said it. Of course I didn't know why Wes was imprisoned. It's something you don't ever ask an ex-con. Everyone knows that much. Basic good manners.

'A disgrace,' said Micky.

'Everyone deserves a second chance,' said Hobbs reasonably. 'But it would be a shame if people were to find out what kind of a person was frying their eggs. Might impact on footfall in a way that could be fairly negative. I guess. Well, au revoir.' He patted my arm.

'You know we shared a cell for a while,' said Micky. He paused, made sure he had my full attention. 'One of the worst crimes there is. He's lucky he's still alive.'

13

HMM

The thing about modern youth is that they always seem so tired. I'm sure we had more energy when we were young. We were always kicking balls or re-enacting *Rollerball* on our choppers, or looking for exciting anti-social behaviour opportunities. Windows to break. Doors to knock and run from. We spent a lot of time roaming backstreets trying to find the newsagents and the off-licences with the doziest – i.e. kindest – staff, so that we could shoplift Texan bars or Marathons without risking capture.

The current lot are always exhausted. Hard to imagine them doing any of that. Zoe would say it's because the grown-up world has made them that way. She would say that the kids are so neglected and bullied by the adults that the entire generation is suffering from a range of stress disorders. They are depressed at having nothing to look forward to. We have replaced dreams with memes and the children don't even know what it is they're missing, but they know there's something and it's making them sick at heart.

They are less innocent than we were and maybe it's true that innocence is energising while knowledge of the way the world works, the futility of it all, is just more draining and harder to live with.

Whatever, this lack of generational oomph meant that when da kidz started to choose the pavement outside Ernies as the place to hang, we didn't worry too much. At first it was just a couple of pink-eyed tykes in stained hoodies, both of them prone to blushing if addressed directly. Easy to disregard. It got more annoying when, day after sodding day, their numbers grew until after a couple of weeks there was an actual picket line of belliger-ent youth lounging outside the cafe attempting to give the hairy eyeball to our customers. It wasn't nice and there didn't seem much we could do about it. Even Wes at his most glowering couldn't get them to move along.

I worried it would affect business but our customers though, they're tough, they just served those attempted death stares right back. That's the thing about Ernies Stonebeck regulars. You can't out-evil them. They don't back down. Not ever. Not one of them. Fact, they seem to like to raise the stakes, if possible.

Our guys all had their own trademarked ways of resisting intimidation too. The two Jennies liked to share a kiss as they walked the idling gauntlet, and this made the hooded toughs shift uneasily. You could see it made them feel a bit funny. Meanwhile baby Eddard learned to give them the finger. He's a bright kid right enough. Quick on the uptake.

Most surprisingly impervious to the pressure was probably Sad Rosie. All five foot nothing of her. She came in every morning, same as she always did, and she walked past the mean boys, head high, mouth as thin as a cut. The lads always recoiled, always moved back a step. It was like they feared her ingrained melancholy suggested witchy superpowers.

No one had ever known Sad Rosie to talk except to order a brew and a scone. She was one of the few regulars who never talked about herself. Everyone else was in the caff because they needed a friendly place to sit, and eventually they all spilt the crucial facts about themselves. I knew more than I needed to about most people who come here. For example, I knew that Chas Diggle had six kids by four different women and didn't see any of them, not kids or women. I knew that the two Jennies were both married to men when they first met, that neither of them had thought they were interested in women in that way but they just got closer and closer until one night, a few ciders in, they just took what seemed a natural next step.

One of the husbands took it well. The other tried to burn his own house down with the two Jennies asleep inside. He's still doing time for it.

What did I know about Ken? I knew that he played professional rugby league for a few seasons. Bradford Northern – a big club back in the day – and I knew that he could do *The Times* crossword in less than half an hour. Even the super-brainy Dr Zoe took longer than that. Though it was true that Ken might struggle with a crossword that was in Hungarian. But that, finally, was what I liked about Stonebeck, I think: that the people could always surprise you. That appearances were nearly always deceptive. That your first impressions were almost always wrong.

It was mostly Zoe who got the goss and then relayed it back to me, but the point is that everyone talked. For most people it's the point of a café. The price of the tea and the coffee is just the rent you pay for having a warm place to share the stories that make up a life.

Rosie never shared her story. She always came in, placed her order in a whisper and sat there on her own for an hour or two, always looking as if she was on the verge of tears. First few weeks we – or another customer – would ask if she was okay and she'd always say that she was, in a tone of real surprise. Of course she was all right. Why would we think otherwise?

So we stopped asking, just started calling her Sad Rosie among ourselves.

Then, one Friday morning, the sky surprisingly blue outside, the radio playing *Say A Little Prayer* and everyone humming along, a woman came up to the counter, ordered a veggie breakfast and glanced around the room looking for a free table. She was about fifty-five, good-looking, well dressed, expensive trainers – and she gasped when she saw Rosie and hurried over to her. She couldn't get there fast enough, actually bumped into tables on the way, tripped over chairs, stumbled into pushchairs, trod on dogs.

'Rosie!' she said. 'Rosie Booker, I can't believe it! It's so good to see you!' Her enthusiasm was obviously genuine, her delight unforced.

From behind the counter I watched as Rosie looked up, startled. Her face broke into a smile of startling warmth. She stood, the two women embraced and then they were talking nineteen to the dozen. The new woman hardly looked up when I brought her food over, but Rosie did another amazing thing, she actually introduced us.

'Luke, this is my old friend Steph. Steph Baber. We were at school together.' She said it with shy pride. 'Luke is the owner here, Steph. Best buns in Yorkshire.'

'Well, I'll have to check that out later.' She arched an eyebrow and Rosie smiled at the innuendo. She really had got a heart-warming grin. This Steph apologised to the whole café about the knocking into their dogs and their kids, but hey, look, this is her good friend Rosie who acted in all the school plays with her, who was a right show-off, got all the leads while she, Steph, had to be content with the supporting cast parts. She told us that Rosie was much desired at school.

'All the boys wanted to shag her, all the girls wanted to be her.' Rosie blushed and the two of them sat and laughed together for a good hour before leaving arm in arm. Steph blew kisses as she left and promised to check out my buns properly next time.

What larks.

There had been a shivery moment ten minutes into her visit when the penny had dropped that this Steph was the lady on the bike, the one that I almost ran over the day that Selena left me. However, she didn't seem to recognise me and I chose not to share the information that I had nearly killed her not too long ago. People can be quite judgemental about that stuff.

We all had a happier day after that. Seeing Rosie come to life like this was hugely uplifting. Every time Zoe and I passed each other we couldn't help smiling. Even Wes and I managed to have a bit of a laugh, and that was good because we'd been awkward with each other since Hobbs had dropped in. When I came to lock up the shop in the evening, the youths had gone.

That night, I met Selena in the city centre. We were going to talk practicalities. She was anyway – I was just going to look at her face. Maybe make her feel bad, by sitting there being all quietly broken.

It was Friday night and raucous. I had to push through streets full of sweary men in suits shouting at each other and the world. All of them thinking they were comic geniuses or that their political opinions and football allegiances needed trumpeting to a grateful nation. The thoroughfares of the city seemed full of marauding stag parties. Made me nervous. There should be a law. I've often thought that men should be banned from going out in single-sex groups of more than three. Everyone would have a better time, men and women.

The gin bar we met in was okay though, I suppose. Boringly contemporary in the black and chrome manner of the twenty-first-century city-centre hang-out, but the ridiculous prices meant that it was only half-full and we found a table quickly. I was determined not to start an argument and I think Selena had made the same resolution, so we were cordial – cordialish – swapping inconsequential chat. We could have been former work colleagues having a catch-up. Made me sad. I felt my resolution to be quietly and nicely sorrowful wobble. Maybe I would be noisily and nastily sorrowful instead.

Selena was not in her business clothes and not wearing her business face. She looked young and cheerful. That also took its toll on my resolution to play nice if I'm honest.

'Do you remember your hen night?' I said.

She grew wary immediately. 'Yes, of course, why?'

'I remember phoning you from my stag do and hearing how you were all having a right laugh. I could hear all that joyful squealing in the background.'

'We were doing all the dances we used to do at school discos.'

'That's right,' I said.

I had phoned home because my stag night, taking place in Liverpool at the same time, had descended into a weary pub crawl – a pub trudge – and the increasingly forced banter had begun to depress my spirits utterly so I had phoned home and heard the girls were throwing the moves they had once done to classic hits. Songs like 'Tiger Feet' and 'Under The Moon of Love' and 'Dancing Queen' and I'd realised what was missing from my own night out. Our stag night was missing hens. It was missing wives and girlfriends. It was missing oestrogen. At that moment I had wanted to be able to teleport back to Selena and her mates.

The reverse was not true of course; the girls' night would not have been enhanced by the sudden appearance of stags. We were a gang of blokes talking shit at the top of our voices because we were fucking lonely and wanting a cuddle and we couldn't admit this to anyone.

Now there was a pause. 'Why did you mention the hen night?' Selena asked.

The hen night, note, not *my* hen night. It had become impersonal. Like the whole do was accidental. Or like it was weather. Like you say *the* storm, not *my* storm. *The* hurricane not *my* hurricane.

'No reason,' I said.

I wanted to tell her about my plans to outlaw gangs of blokes, to stop them roaming free range through the city. I wanted to tell her how vulnerable I had felt coming through the city centre just now. I wanted her to snort and wave a dismissive hand and tell me I was ridiculous. I wanted us to be how we were, but I just couldn't see how to get us there.

We drank in silence for a bit, we did very two-star chit-chat until eventually Selena said that she'd heard I'd had an offer for Ernies.

'That's right,' I said. 'A very good offer. I turned it down.'

'I heard that too. Why?'

'Because I like my café. I like working there and I don't like the guy making an offer. He's a bully. Plus he called me Lukey. How did you hear anyway?'

'The business community in this city is small and the developments around Southside are quite exciting. It's a hot topic of conversation. He really called you Lukey? God.'

I bloody knew it. 'We're actually calling it that now? Southside?'

'Just a name,' she said. 'And if the place loses its stigma and property prices go up, that's a good thing, right?'

'Not necessarily,' I said

There was another pause. I sipped my gin. Nowt special about it except the price and the fact it came with some complementary beetroot crisps in a little china pot. Beetroot crisps. World's gone mad.

'Luke, look . . .' She stopped. I'm reminded suddenly of school. I had a teacher once – I can't remember his name – who thought it was hilarious to parody a road safety campaign of the time whenever he addressed me: 'Stop, Luke and Listen' he would say. Every lesson without fail, sometimes twice or three times a lesson, even if I hadn't said anything. Even if I was concentrating hard. And the class would snigger dutifully. Every time. Fucking collaborators.

'I need you to sell the business and the house or both,' Selena said. 'I've quit my job and . . .' She trailed off, looked away.

And what? Oh, yes. The gap year with the toyboy ponce.

'Romeo has debts, I suppose,' I said.

It was a guess, but an inspired one. She flushed. 'We just want to get on with things.'

'Yes, time's running out for you, isn't it?'

She said that she didn't know why I was being so arsey. 'Why don't you start dating again? You might enjoy it.'

'I'm married,' I said.

'Separated,' she said. 'Getting a divorce.'

'Yes, I'm told that I'm very divorceable.'

There wasn't much to say after that. We sipped in silence. We finished the crisps. The barman came over and took our glasses. He asked if he could get us anything.

I gave him my theory that the rise in the drinking of craft gins parallels the rise of a toxic English nationalism. I told him to think about it. People see gin as quintessentially English – even though it's Dutch – and it's interesting that everyone wants to drink it now. I said that it's fascinating how bars like his have appeared in the last ten years. Told him that gin-drinking and singing about the Second World War at the football and beating the shit out of foreigners every chance we get are all part of the same wave. The wave that had brought us all those British backs against the wall movies that fetishise Churchill and our finest fucking hour. A finest hour that only happened because of incompetence, cowardice and idleness in the British officer class.

'Drinking gin is a racist act,' I said now. 'Nationalistic at the very least. No getting away from it.'

There was a silence. He had no idea what I was talking about.

'I think we're good,' Selena said, and minutes later I was out in the noisy streets pushing past all the Friday night gorillas and wanting to punch every single one of them in their stupid red and laughing faces. Yes, there should definitely be a law.

On Monday, the tired youth were back in place and Rosie was also back to her old sad self. Worse if anything. She mouthed her order for tea and a scone and sat by the window, head lowered looking like she was about to cry, and steadfastly refused any efforts to engage her in conversation. We really tried, too. We talked about how great Steph seemed, we asked when they last saw each other and when they were going to meet again, we asked if Rosie had ever thought about getting involved in any theatre groups round here. Nothing.

In the end we just left her alone with her scone and her thoughts since it was so obviously what she wanted. Depressing, and Team Ernies ended up getting irritable with each other again, seemed to get under each other's feet. I kept wondering what it was Wes did to get sent down in a way I hadn't since the first days he worked here. I had told Hobbs and his goon that I didn't care what it was but I was beginning to wonder if that was true. There are some debts to society that you can never repay.

The mood in the café was not helped by the fact that across the alley the words that had been on the wall forever and which we all found uplifting – NVR FORGET HOW BEAUTIFUL YOU ARE – had been painted over. The new slogan – WE'RE WATCHING YOU SKUM – was somehow nowhere near as inspirational. I suppose we should have been reassured by the fact that at least they'd got the apostrophe right, even if the spelling was off.

Selena called just before closing, to tell me off. To wag her finger at me. 'We have to stay civil with each other, you know, Luke. For the kids, if nothing else.'

'Like you said, they're grown-ups now.' Childish to parrot her own words back at her, I know, and I heard her sigh. 'Anyway,' I said, 'I thought it was a pretty civil meeting, as these things go.'

She didn't argue. 'Have you heard from Grace at all?' she said instead.

'She checks in.'

'What does she say about uni?'

'She says it's going well. She's enjoying it. Seems to be studying hard, making friends. She's having fun, I think.'

'You don't think that's weird?'

Come to think of it, it was weird. Grace had hated high school. She did okay in the end but had to be nagged and cajoled and bribed into doing any work. From the age of fourteen onwards we were paying her a fiver for every paragraph of completed homework. Cost a fortune. She particularly hated her A levels, was always moaning about how boring the books were, how stressy her teachers were. Was always threatening to quit and get a job in a shop.

Her final grades were not amazing. Just good enough. I think she only got those because for the six weeks before the exams we grounded her and even made her earn time alone with her phone by studying, which she had to do at the kitchen table where we could see her. It was a dismal few weeks but it did the trick. Yet at Sussex, with no one to push her or to take her devices away from her, she seemed to be doing splendidly. Either our tactics last year were unnecessarily draconian then (which is what Grace had said at some volume over and over every day of those nightmare weeks) or she'd had a dramatic change in her whole attitude to study.

'Maybe she really has just caught maturity,' I said now. 'Or maybe she's being properly stretched at last. Perhaps she was just bored at school, wasn't being stimulated enough?'

'Maybe,' said Selena. 'It's a theory, I suppose.' She wasn't convinced and, if I'm honest, neither was I.

'We should go down to see her,' I said. 'A surprise visit.'

'I'm not sure,' Selena said.

'Come on, like you said, it'll be good for her to see that her parents are civilised.'

'Can we manage it though: civilised? For a whole day? In Brighton?'

'Of course we can.'

'Hmm.'

I knew better than to ask what hmm meant. I knew already. Everyone does: hmm always means 'you're talking absolute cock, mate', but then Selena surprised me by saying, 'Maybe you're right. Maybe we should go down.'

There was a pause then she told me she didn't want Grace getting the wrong idea, didn't want her thinking that we were getting back together.

'No, because that would be a terrible thing, wouldn't it?'

Another pause and then she made a conversational swerve, one that was also meant to be a conciliatory gesture. She said that she thought I was probably right not to rush into selling Ernies to Tony Hobbs.

'I asked around and he does seem to be a nasty piece of work. But you need to do something. See a bank, Luke, find out what your options are because burying your head in the sand is not one of them. If you don't find another way of raising the cash, we might have to take Hobbs's money.'

'Hobbs's dirty money,' I said. I was thinking that she was wrong anyway. Burying your head in the sand is always an option. A lot of things do just go away if you ignore them long enough.

'Luke.' There was a warning in her voice.

'Okay,' I said, quickly. I was too tired for a row now. 'I'll see an Independent Financial Adviser. Really soon.'

'Really? You promise?'

'Cross my heart.'

'Hmm,' she said.

14

PEBBLES AND FISH

The kids had been talking and, like Selena, they had decided that I needed to start dating again. I went to see Charlie play rugby and in the pub after the game he said, 'You've got to get back out there, Dad. You've got to get back on the bike.'

I went down to Brighton to take Grace shopping, and over the world's most expensive macaroni cheese she said, 'Plenty more fish in the sea, Dad. Plenty more pebbles on the beach.'

I love my kids. They are kind, considerate and smart. It is true that they may not be the most original thinkers though.

Nevertheless, I endured a lecture from the dentist and another from the barber. I bought a new mustard-coloured jacket from M & S. I even invested in condoms. Viagra too. Those little blue coffins promising all the backup an ageing lover might need. Well, you never know. Pays to be prepared, though I nearly didn't bother. No prescription for Viagra needed these days but – like the dentist, like the barber – the pharmacist also felt duty-bound to deliver a sermon before handing over the goods. A homily delivered in a room about the size of the toilet stall in Ernies. Him on one plastic chair, me on the other, so close that our knees were almost touching, so close I could smell his sweat and see the little clumps of bristles under his chin that he'd missed while shaving. These were the things I concentrated on while he gave me a finger-waggy list of warnings about thrombosis and renal failure and the need to make sure I had a full medical check-up in the next six months. A proper road test. He seemed very disapproving of the whole idea of people like me having sex at all. Nearly put me off the whole business before I had even started.

Nevertheless, every Thursday for the next few weeks I met up with strangers in a variety of city-centre café-bars. It was a bit like going on an evening course in a subject I had flunked at school. In fact, I'd have had more luck going on an actual evening course. Home maintenance for beginners. Website design 101. How to research your family history. I'd have got more action at any of these.

It did not go well, let's put it like that.

I made every mistake going. I did learn a lot though. Mostly I learned that dating – always a dangerous sport – is way more brutal these days than it was in the past. That there were a lot of other things to worry about before you got to possible sildenafil citrate induced renal failure.

This is the modern world all over, isn't it? Things are invented which seem to promise to make life easier before it turns out that we've just added a layer of complication to our lives. Thorny, almost insoluble, etiquette problems for a start.

Before I met Selena, my relationships had all begun in the pub with people I already knew. You'd go out with people from work, you'd get hammered and sometimes you'd end up sleeping with one of them. If that happened a few times, well, you could probably assume that you were now in some kind of relationship.

111

Sometime after that – maybe a few weeks, or months – you might have a discussion about the nature of this relationship. Were you officially boyfriend/girlfriend and therefore exclusive and not about to fall into bed with someone else? Or were you friends with benefits – fuck buddies – to use my kids' charming phrase, and so free to continue the haphazard search for The One while still getting off with each other after an SWD?

These days you download an app or three. You share your most appealing, most carefully spontaneous selfie and your most cheerfully non-threatening bio and, if anyone likes them then you might meet for cocktails and beetroot crisps somewhere. You meet in public, you let people know where you're going and you have mates ready to call you with a family emergency needing your help if they get a text asking for rescue.

In theory it's much better than the old ways. More civilised. In practice it is way more awkward. For a start when you get there you have to make proper convers-ation rather than just get the drinks in and let alcohol lead you by the hand to the gutter or the stars, or wher-ever else it wants to take you.

I'm not blaming any of the women. They all seemed all right. More than all right. Too good for most blokes. Too good for me. All nice, all good-looking and all pretty sorted. They all reminded me of Selena actually. Which didn't help. So yes, I know, the problem was definitely mine not theirs. I hold my hand up. All me.

Or, rather, the fault was mostly mine. It was mostly me. I hold my hand halfway up. Charlie and Grace played their parts too. In at least three instances I tripped up because I was badly advised by my children.

Whatever, all my dates – except one – finished in under an hour and here are the reasons I was given. I'll be brief because I can't bear to dwell on it all.

There was the date – my first in thirty-two years – where I was so nervous that I literally couldn't speak for the first twenty minutes – twenty minutes where I went to the toilet at least four times. The last time I came back and found that my date had gone, leaving a fiver and a note. The note said to never contact her again, her time was precious, she had had to get a babysitter for this. Fair enough, I suppose.

There was the date which finished because 'you're always on your phone'. This was Grace's fault because she kept texting to see how things were going and I felt I had to reply in case she assumed silence meant that it was going badly.

There was date that ended because 'you did a mid-date review'. (I just asked how she thought it was going so far and then offered my own opinion when she struggled for an answer.)

There was the date that finished because 'you slagged off your ex'.

The date that finished because 'you went on about how great your ex is'.

The date that finished because 'you're not actually six foot, are you?'

I blame Charlie for this one. He said five foot ten was near enough to six foot and that girls expected you to finesse this stuff. He said that if I said I was five ten they'd assume that I was really five eight and who wants to go out with a short-arse?

Charlie himself is six foot two. He thinks almost everyone is a short-arse.

Similarly, there was the date that finished because 'you're not really forty-nine, are you?' This one was Grace's bad. She said women think men over fifty are generally past it, and you'll agree that I had my own very good reasons for thinking she might be right about this.

Turns out women are even less tolerant of liars than they are of the short and the old. Who knew?

The last date I had before I gave up was the only one to go on until closing time. Eleanor Steele is a Director of Services for the council. Culture. Something like that. We had similar politics. We had the same taste in books and music. She was excited by the fact I ran a café. Most of the men she'd met up to then had been mortgage brokers, solicitors, recruitment consultants and sundry other desk-bound losers. We had a laugh. But still, this didn't lead to a second date because, and I swear this is true, 'you insisted on paying and I don't like controlling men'.

Which seems harsh. It's not like I had really wanted to pay. Just thought it was what you did.

So those are the mistakes I made, all of them basic, apparently. Schoolboy errors. Except I'm sure your actual schoolboys are completely across this stuff these days. They probably teach it in school now. Dating etiquette as part of compulsory citizenship courses now along with pension planning. Whatever, my failure in this department knocked my confidence a bit.

I confided my lack of progress to Zoe. She was as unsurprised as she was unsympathetic. She asked me exactly how long I had been with Selena. I told her. Thirty-one years, I said.

'Of course dating isn't working out,' she said. 'You're nowhere near ready.'

She told me her theory which was that for every year a couple was together it would take them at least a month to get over any break-up. She said it was a foolproof and absolutely scientific equation.

'So you're saying I have to wait thirty-one months before I get back out there?' I said.

114

'At least,' she said.

'So I'll be ready to date . . .' I tried to do the maths. Couldn't. Gave up.

Zoe laughed. I pointed out that Selena didn't seem to have waited any months at all.

Zoe disagreed. 'She probably started getting over you at least thirty months ago. She did her grieving for the death of the marriage while she was still in it. Oh, and now you're going to storm out again. Your problem is that you can't handle the truth, Luke Greenwood!'

She had to shout this last sentence because I was already on my way out of the door. I stopped, took a breath, turned to face her, forced myself to speak slowly, calmly.

'No. For your information, Doctor Vargo, I am merely on my way to the Spar to get more bread.'

'Yeah, right.'

I got bread. When I came back I put the loaves in the freezer because – of course – we did have loads of bread already, though Zoe was sensitive enough to not point this out. I resolved to take her advice and not attempt to date again for a year or three. I found I was not actually that upset by this. I was fine with it.

That night I phoned Charlie and told him that I'd get back on the bike when the new bruises from falling off this time round had healed. Then I spoke to Grace, informed her that all the pebbles and all the fish had turned out to be inadequate replacements for her mother.

Neither of them argued. Grace seemed to want to say something, seemed to have other things on her mind.

'Dad,' she said.

'What?' I said, possibly a little belligerently. I was in a bad mood, I admit it.

'Nothing,' she said. 'Nothing.'

*   *   *

You know the saddest thing? The person I really wanted to talk to about my dating disasters, the person who'd be most entertained by them, the person who would make me see how daft it was to take this stuff seriously?

Selena.

15

PUBLIC DISPLAYS
OF AFFECTION

Last thing on a Friday and Wes suggested that he and I have a swift half in The Swan. Said he needed to have a word with me about something.

My heart sank. When someone wants a word it's never good news, is it? To be honest, I wasn't sure I even wanted to do small talk with Wes right then, never mind a heart-to-heart. I was finding I couldn't really deal with him at all. Hadn't been doing the bags-and-pads boxing sessions. Could hardly even look at him.

Wouldn't have been so awkward if Zoe was coming but she'd already knocked off early, saying she had a doctor's appointment.

My worries about Wes's past crimes had been growing. Started to get obsessive. I'd done some pretty extensive googling and at first it was a relief that Wes's name hadn't come up, though later I realised that anyone who does anything properly heinous obviously changes their name, so the lack of hits might well actually be a bad sign.

Pitts's insinuation had been that Wes was a nonce, but it was hard to believe. Yes, I know that nonces don't have horns and cloven hoofs. I know that they look just like you and me, that they have normal faces and normal jobs and that they can hide in plain sight. I know all of that. But Wes? Really? Just couldn't imagine it.

Still, it nagged at me. Had become an itch I had to scratch.

We didn't talk much on the way to the pub. A bit of desultory football chat. The wrong managers picking the wrong players, all of whom were paid too much. Better than silence, but not much.

In The Swan nothing had changed since the last time we were in. Really, nothing. It was like everyone had been in suspended animation, only coming to a kind of life the moment we walked through the door. There was the same path-lab light, the same tired bartender in his same T-shirt, reading the same tabloid. It even looked like it had the same headline. Something about some TV presenter caught drink-driving.

The customers too were the same. The same puffy white faces staring morosely into the same smeary glasses of urine-coloured lager. I know that pub regulars must think, feel, love, hate, laugh just like we all do, but sometimes it is hard to believe it. There was the same smell of stale potato snacks. The same plaintively bombastic music playing. One pint, I vowed to myself, one pint and then I was out of there.

While Wes got the drinks, I thought back to when I hired him. Remembered the first conversation about him with Malika Burns.

Malika was his probation officer. She used to come in to Ernies for a brew and beans on toast. Probation officers, like cops and paramedics and other frontline public service grunts, often find themselves round our way. They make up a good proportion of business at Ernies. I think it was for the probation officers that I first started ordering in the almond milk. Probation officers and social workers are always early adopters when it comes to food fads.

Anyway, there was a day when she came in and we were struggling. The last cook had walked out and Malika mentioned that she had a client – decent bloke, quiet, hard-working – who had been training as a chef inside. Had been acing it, top grades for everything. Could fry an egg like a dream, his béchamel an actual symphony, that kind of thing. I asked then what he'd done to end up inside and she'd said she couldn't tell me – it wasn't really the done thing – but that she was certain that he would be very safe in a café environment. There was no history of violence.

I asked Zoe what she thought.

'When's he out?' she said.

'Tomorrow, actually,' Malika said.

'Well, let's throw him in at the deep end then,' Zoe said. 'I don't think Ernies can cope with many more days with Luke as head chef.'

So Wes came straight from the slammer to the caff and he was as good as Malika had said. He was quick, unflappable and clean which are the things you most need in any kitchen, particularly in a rough-and-ready diner like ours. And I liked him. We got on.

More importantly – and more surprisingly – Zoe had liked him straight away too and she likes almost no one. She pronounced him 'sound' which is the very highest possible praise in her lexicon. Also, I guess we both liked the fact that by hiring an ex-con we were doing A Good Thing.

That was four years ago and we'd been a great team, but now I was growing convinced I'd have to fire him. However good he'd been for the caff, I just couldn't have someone working for me that I, in the normal scheme of things, wouldn't even serve.

Obviously I'd let him put his side of things first, but I had a bad feeling.

Right then the person I felt saddest for was Zoe. I thought this might really do her head in. Over the last couple of weeks it had become clear that love was in the air in Ernies. Wes and Zoe had begun not to care who knew they were an item. They held hands, they called each other honey and darling in a way that was meant to be ironic but sort of clearly wasn't, and they couldn't stop smooching in the caff. People had commented. Chas Diggle said all this kissing put him off his breakfast. Zoe just laughed at him.

'Not one for a PDA then, Chas?' she'd said.

'A what?'

'A Public Display of Affection.'

'No one likes it,' he'd said.

'I do. I love a PDA, me. I want to see the whole world snogging all the time.' She had looked thoughtful then. 'You know, I think snogging is my favourite English word.'

We supped in silence. Minutes passed. Wes had suggested this pint, surely it was up to him to start talking? We heard the whole of 'I Will Always Love You', the whole of 'Everything I Do, I Do for You'. I wondered how much more I could take.

'God, this place could badly use some disco,' Wes said. Then, 'Do you know why Zoe's at the doctor's?'

It was suddenly clear to me. Oh God.

'Yeah, reckons she's pregnant,' he said.

'Bit early to say, isn't it?'

'That's what I said, but she's pretty certain.'

'She's right about most things,' I said.

'Yep,' he said. 'Yep, she is.'

Except in her choice of blokes, I thought. Her track record there was poor.

We sat in silence for a while until I remembered what you were meant to say at times like these. I offered congratulations.

Wes smiled faintly. 'Thanks.'

We talked a little about children. Or I did. How much they cost but how rewarding they were. Banalities. Platitudes. Wes nodded and murmured along, but I knew he was not really listening. Which was reasonable enough, even I wasn't really listening. Instead, as I was gabbing on I was just thinking, oh Christ, that poor kid. Thinking how its only hope was if Zoe ended up a single parent. Eventually he cut in and stopped me.

'So. Cards on the table time,' he said.

This is it, I thought. This is where he tells me what he was in for. This is where he throws himself on my mercy, claims that he is utterly rehabilitated and, while he agrees it was a sickening crime, swears he's genuinely cured, genuinely wanting a fresh start. He's going to ask me to take pity on him. He'll urge me to think of Zoe, to think of the baby.

I'm prepared to be reasonable, I think. But he's got to be properly upfront. He can't sanitise whatever it is he's done. Can't hold anything back. He's also got to show proper remorse and some evidence that he's still doing work on himself. He's got to prove to me that he's got support in place to keep on the straight and narrow. And of course he's got to tell Zoe all the details too. Let her make an informed decision about whether to continue the relationship.

'Thing is, Luke,' he began, then paused. Took another sip of his murky IPA. There was Queen on the radio now. Freddie Mercury was saying how I was his best friend.

'Thing is,' Wes said. 'I'm going to need more money.'

'What?' I was wrong-footed, blindsided.

'I've been on nine quid an hour for four years now. And with a kid on the way, like . . .' He trailed off.

'You brought me here to ask for a pay rise?'

'Yeah.' He seemed puzzled. 'It's fair enough to ask, isn't it?'

121

'I suppose,' I said. And then I said it. Just blurted it out. Told him that I'd thought he was going to tell me why he'd gone to prison. Told him that I'd been thinking about sacking him.

'What the fuck for?'

I told him what Micky Pitts had said, about how it had been preying on my mind.

'You think I'm a nonce? Stand up.' His voice was mild. His eyes steady on mine. They were cool. No heat in them. Almost colourless. He took another pull at his pint.

'What?' I said.

'I asked you to stand up, Luke.' And, despite being fairly sure it was a bad idea, I did it. Couldn't tell you why. I stood up and – of course – he smacked me hard in the face. Twice. He was clinical about it too. Two short, hard, fast jabs. The first one caught me on the nose and the second one right in the mouth and I was suddenly sprawled amid the tables and the stools. The noise was strangely musical, a glissando, like a car hitting a greenhouse.

Have you ever been hit in the face by a proper boxer? By someone who knows exactly what they're doing? I advise against it. There was the metal taste of blood in my mouth, a ringing in my ears, a tinnitus that was surely permanent, and I was blinded by hot tears.

I was stunned enough to stay where I was for a while. I'm not sure how long. Could have been a minute, could have been thirty minutes. Could have been an entire fucking lifetime.

When I got myself together enough to struggle back up to the banquette, my head was banging. This was a headache that was making itself comfortable, was settling in for days. This was likely to turn into a migraine that was in no hurry to move on, was going to stick around.

Wes had gone. The barman wandered over to pick up the stools and to half-heartedly sweep up glass. He didn't ask how I was.

I leaned back against the sticky vinyl of the banquette, closed my eyes. There were painful lights dancing between my eyes and lids. I ran my tongue over my teeth. Seemed like they were all still there which was something. I closed my eyes, concentrated on the colours dancing there. Quite pretty really. Almost psychedelic.

When I opened my eyes again it was to find Zoe sitting on a stool across the table, a glass of fizzy water in front of her. Which I guessed meant that the doctor had confirmed the pregnancy.

'You've got blood on your face,' she said, and handed me a hankie. It was not too clean but I used it anyway.

'Your boyfriend is a psycho,' I said.

It hurt to speak. Felt like even this short sentence had somehow ripped open a new wound in my mouth. Had seeded a major ulcer there.

'Not really,' she said. 'Just pissed off. He phoned me, told me what you said. Seems to me like you had it coming. If you were really that interested in Wes's criminal past you could have asked me, you know. Wes might have been a bit shy, but I'd have told you. Do you want me to tell you now?'

'Not really.'

She told me anyway.

According to Zoe, Wes had developed a gambling habit a few years back. Began with a weekly and modest flutter on the horses and progressed until it became several hours a day in front of a fixed-odds terminal losing money way beyond anything that his job at the time could support. It was a decent job too, logistics manager at a distribution warehouse somewhere off the M62.

As he'd got deeper in he'd become close to his ninety-year-old neighbour, a woman whose eyesight and hearing were going, who was gradually but definitely losing her marbles, whose kids and grandkids didn't come round very often, who had grown increasingly reliant on the quiet, handsome and thoroughly charming bloke next door. This lady – a Mrs Calder – was always saying how her new friend Wes was her lifeline, her rock, the only thing keeping her going. Nothing was too much trouble. Couldn't do enough. She was lucky to have him looking out for her.

Eventually, however, a child or a grandchild did finally bother to come round, and had discovered a National Savings Bank passbook open in the lounge, picked it up and did the maths. Turned out that Wes had done the old lady out of £50,000 – all of which had gone into those infernal fixed-odds dream machines of Mr Ladbrokes.

The judge in the ensuing court case had taken a dim view of the whole preying on the elderly thing, wasn't impressed by the abuse of trust and all that, and so Wes had got an unusually long sentence for a first-time offender. Eight years.

His solicitor had suggested he could appeal, but Wes hadn't wanted to, had felt he had deserved what he got. Was too overcome with shame to even think about trying to reduce his sentence.

'It's a nice story,' I said.

'You think that's a nice story?'

'Nicer than being a paedo. But why should I believe it?'

'You should believe it because it's me telling you, Luke. I don't lie. You should know that about me. You should . . .'

Zoe's voice drifted away, dissipated into the ready-salted air of the The Swan. She sighed, pushed her hand through her hair in the way that she had and produced an envelope from her bag. The sigh, the hand through the hair, the irritated way she rooted about in her bag, all of it told me she didn't like me very much at that moment. Fact, she was thinking I was a bit of a tosser. Just another stupid man among all the other stupid men she'd had to deal with in her life. From Budapest to here, just one disappointment after another.

She shoved the envelope across to me. Inside was a worn and fragile cutting from a national rag. The same story was told there and the photo that accompanied it was definitely Wes, though the name was different.

'Thing is, Luke, even if he *had* been a paedophile, even if he'd been a rapist or a murderer he would still have served his time. Would still be entitled to work.'

'Yeah, I guess.'

'No I guess about it. You judge a society by how it treats its criminals, and you judge a person by how much ordinary human kindness they show to those who have messed up.'

So that was me stubbed out. They should have Zoe on Thought for the bloody Day.

She finished off by reminding me how the business class work. How they divide us against each other in the interests of making profits for themselves. White against black, North against South, old against young, men against women, likes of me against likes of Wes, all of it serving the continuing accumulation of wealth by a global class of selfish wankers. In this case the whole game just served the accumulation of Ernies by Hobbs. In other words, she took some time to explain – at length – that I was being taken for a ride, that I was being comprehensively mugged off. That she'd thought I was brighter than to fall for the basic capitalist playbook.

Never mind mansplaining, the young of both sexes bloody love to youthsplain.

I was in the middle of thanking her for pointing all this out to me when my phone fanfared inside my pocket. Grace. In tears. I could hardly hear her through the sobs. My heart contracted. My mouth dried. My blood chilled. No one ever gets used to hearing their children weep.

'Dad? Dad? It's Charlie. Something's happened. You need to be here.'

16

THESE CASES CAN BE
VERY COMPLEX

We were standing around Charlie's hospital bed. He was still and silent in an artificial coma, and all strapped up. Spine held in place by metal braces. Tubes running into his arm. There was a nurse, her movements efficient and brisk. She checked things, finger tap-tap-tapping at her tablet. She reminded me of young Eddard, child of the two Jennies. The same level of fierce concentration. She consulted dials and switches. Her face a busy mime, a silent film. She nodded, frowned, generally shaped her face to make it look as if important stuff was going on. She was an explorer, an astronaut on some spacewalk business. Information must be discovered, recorded, processed. Machinery must be monitored.

None of us – myself, Selena, Grace and an uncomfortable probationary copper called Lauren – made a sound. We had run out of conversation a while back. We held paper cups of a lukewarm drink that vaguely resembled tea. It was our third cup. The room smelled of air freshener and worry, because yes, worry has a smell: sweat and dying flowers. Tainted water.

We were bored too. We wanted something to happen, but we were terrified about what that something might turn out to be.

Somewhere outside the room I could hear masculine laughter. I imagined heavy-handed flirtation between porters and nurses. Gallows humour. Imitations of pompous doctors. Tales of japes with bandages and embalming fluid. Lauren's eyes flickered towards the door, you just knew she would rather be out there participating in that ponderous jesting rather than here in this oppressive silence. Of course she would. Who wouldn't? She caught me looking at her and blushed. I wanted to tell her that it was okay, that I would also rather be out there with the nurses and the porters. I'd rather be listening to the crap corpse jokes. But I didn't.

Charlie had a fractured spine. Group of blokes out on the piss. Aggro in the street after closing time. Random viciousness because one bloke didn't like another bloke's face. Or the way he walked. Or because he was wearing the wrong scarf, had the wrong accent, the wrong laugh. Someone looking at someone funny. No real reasons. Another boring story, something that happens every day, in every town in the country.

I remember Zoe telling me once that men are afraid that women will laugh at them but that women are afraid men will kill them. A quote from some writer or other. Looking down at my son lying in that bed, I wanted to say to her what I hadn't said then because I didn't want a row. Wanted to say, yes, Zoe, what you say is true but you have to remember that men are also afraid that men will kill them. The things that women have to do – cross the road if there's a bloke behind them, keep an eye over their shoulder, maintain a state of hyper-vigilance, be ready to run, keep an improvised weapon to hand, your keys maybe, avoid dark alleyways, take detours round groups of lads – men on their own do this too. Every bloke I have ever known has been attacked by other blokes at some time or other. It's never a square go either,

it's always at least three blokes on one. Men can be fuck-
ers, to each other just as much as to women and children.
If they get the opportunity then fucked-up men will
belittle, beat and kill other men. Doesn't have to be
women and kids.

There was a thing on the radio the other day: 88 per
cent of violent offenders are men and so are 77 per cent of
the victims. The vicious dudes aren't keeping it just
among themselves either. No, the violent are attracted to
the peaceable the way foxes are attracted to hens.

I thought again about the noisy reptiles, the half-cut
raptor-packs that I'd had to push through that night I
met up with Selena for gin and crisps. Thought of my
plan for making blokes go out in mixed groups or not at
all. How we could agitate for that to happen. I thought
about asking the nervous young policewoman what
she thought and then I looked at her blanched face. She
wasn't going to be up to any serious discussions of what
we do about street thuggery. She looked like she was
going to puke, to be honest.

Later there was a frustrating talk in an airless committee
room with another twitchy nurse. She was young too.
Probably not much older than my wife's lover. She introduced herself in a whisper. Call me Gina. She scratched
her neck, pulled at her nose, sniffed. Her eyes were liquid.
Her distress should have been frightening, I suppose,
should have been a harbinger of very bad news – like a
panicking flight attendant on a turbulent flight – but I
didn't mind it. It did scare me, but it was also good to
know we were dealing with a human being.

She listed the results of the preliminary investigations
and asked if we had any questions. Yes, we had a couple
of minor ones: will he walk again? Will he talk again?
Turned out these were the very questions young Gina

129

couldn't – or wouldn't – answer. She batted them away. Too early to say at this stage. These cases can be very complex. There's a lot we don't know about injuries to the brain and the spine. Anyway, they'd have a clearer idea when they'd had a chance to examine the X-rays and the ultrasound. When they'd had a chance to examine the blood tests. Everything that could be done was being done.

We'd been moping about the hospital for a couple of hours when my dad arrived, flustered and angry.

First thing he did was pick a fight with the ward receptionist about hospital car parking charges. 'Daylight bloody robbery. Clement Attlee must be turning in his bloody grave.'

Having missed the consultant's feedback session he went off to hunt her down and returned half an hour later fuming about jumped-up little Hitlers.

'Bloody doctors who look like they should be in high school lecturing me about manners. I told her though, I said they should remember who pays their bloody wages.'

My dad had been drawing a pension for twenty years. He hadn't been paying any doctors any wages for decades.

'Nice one, Dad. You've alienated the hospital staff. Genius move,' I said.

His response to that was to start a row with Selena and I about our separation.

'When is this stupidity going to end?' is how he put it. 'Look at the trouble it's caused.' As if the assault that had landed Charlie here had been brought about by our marital discord. Some kind of karmic retribution. We had torn apart the established order of things and now chaos had begun to reign as we should have known it would.

130

Selena tried to shut him up by saying that it was complicated, and he snorted.

'Marriage isn't bloody rocket science, my dear. It's more like cross-country running.'

He meant you just keep going, one foot in front of the other whatever the terrain, whatever the weather. However miserable it gets, however much the mud sucks at your shoes and however much the rain and wind chills you, however much your wet shorts chafe at your groin, you don't give up. You complete the course.

All right for him to say. Dad had always loved running. Even now, deep into his eighties he limped stiffly around the Park Run course every Saturday. Never came last either. Hard for him to imagine that there were people who would never contemplate putting themselves through that.

'Selena has got herself someone else,' I said.

I didn't look at her but I knew that Selena was turning blazing eyes on me. I felt sick at myself. My stomach cramped. My skin prickled.

'Oh, Dad,' said Grace, and I felt worse but I tried to tough it out.

'What?' I said. 'What?'

My voice sounded tinny and thin even to me.

The laughing voices from the corridors seemed to have stopped now. The machines didn't seem to hum quite so much. A deep silence had settled on the ward.

'So she's had a fling, so what?' Dad said. 'Who hasn't?'

'You haven't,' I said. 'Mum didn't.'

I knew as soon as I said it that I was wrong. He had. Mum did. This was confirmed by his silence.

'I don't believe you,' I said. But I did.

'Oh, Luke, grow up,' he said. In a few brisk sentences he expanded on his blueprint for a long-lasting marriage. It boiled down to this: don't ask, don't tell and just don't bloody get divorced whatever the provocations or the temptations. Oh, and you keep some secrets. This modern taste for getting everything out in the open, it just causes trouble.

'Quite the lifestyle guru, aren't you, Dad?' I said.

'You're not too big for a clip round the ear,' he said.

'Yes, I am,' I said.

'Oh, for God's sake,' said Selena. She left the room, her hand to her eyes. There was a silence. Which is when Grace chose to drop her bombshell.

Since the start of term she'd been to a grand total of three lectures. She'd completed half an essay and, after the Dean of Students had given her a serious pep talk about shaping up or shipping out, she had decided – after careful consideration – that shipping out was probably best for all concerned. Shaping up seemed like a whole lot of wasted effort, she said. 'I never wanted to go to bloody university anyway. It was you and Mum that wanted that.'

As an afterthought she told us that even though she'd quit uni after just a few weeks she had still managed to spend her entire loan.

'I better go and find your mother,' I said.

'Great,' said Grace.

'I won't be long,' I said.

'Take as long as you need,' said Dad. 'We're not going anywhere. Just sort it out. Time the two of you started thinking about your family, started putting them first.'

Selena was at the front of the hospital smoking. This was something she hadn't done for fifteen years. She had always been a tactical smoker really. A pragmatic puffer rather than a compulsive one. Never really an addict. Most people smoke at college and give it up later when adult concerns – health, family, finance – kick in. In

132

contrast, Selena never smoked at college, but took it up when she started working because of the inside intelligence you could gather about a company while standing with the other smokers. Bonding as a band of outlaws in the dedicated smokers' room and later, as the regulations tightened, in doorways, you became privy to the important info about how things really were.

At every company she worked for the smokers constituted an important networking group. The smokers were carrying out permanent SWOT analysis. And, of course, those who smoked were more fun than those who didn't. That was a consideration too.

Still, like everyone, she gave it up in the end. It wasn't the pictures of the blackened lungs and cancerous throats on the fag packets that made Selena quit. Instead, she just got bored of it. The fun people started giving up until one day it was just her and the ham-faced dinosaurs standing in the drizzle making conversation. The quality of the intelligence you could gather deteriorated too. The people in the know were now in the gym and not on the pavement in the rain.

She'd given up easily. Couple of tetchy weeks and it was done with. She moved on. She left smoking without much of a backward glance. Selena is one of those people good at doing things and also good at stopping doing things.

I guessed the fag now was a way of keeping people away. Someone just standing thinking gets asked if they're okay; a person smoking, they're invisible.

Even in the midst of the misery of Charlie's accident I was heartened by the sight of her smoking. It implied that what is dropped can be picked up again when the moment is right. If you can return to cigarettes with all their inconvenient side effects, then why can't you do the same with your husband?

I embraced her. She relaxed into the hug for a second. She smelled of an unfamiliar perfume as well as smoke. The new scent was heavy and muskily sweet.

We stayed wrapped in each other for a long time. We fitted together easily and comfortably. Without thinking about it I stroked her hair, kissed her neck. Her hips shifted. She didn't pull away. I tightened the embrace. We stayed like this for a moment longer.

'Luke,' she said after a while, her voice a whisper. 'What are you doing?'

'Shush,' I said. 'Shush.' I pressed my lips against her neck again. Breathed in that rich new fragrance.

She broke the embrace, took a step back, and flicked her cig onto the ground with an angry gesture. She looked me straight in the eyes. 'It's not happening,' she said.

'What?' I say. 'What's not happening?'

'Do I have to spell it out?' She was annoyed. She kept her eyes on mine.

'Yeah, you probably do,' I said.

She sighed, looked away. Took a breath. Made a visible effort to control herself. 'We aren't going to get back together, Luke. We aren't going to have any just-for-old-times'-sake shags either. We aren't going to be comforting each other by having sex because we're lonely or because our boy is lying in hospital. And it's nothing to do with Jacob either. Jacob wasn't the reason we split up. He was just the explosive that bust a hole in the prison wall.'

'You weren't in a prison.'

'Yes, I was. I was in a bloody cage. It wasn't your fault. You didn't make the cage, I made it myself. Built it bit by bit. I allowed my life to become a cell. That's my responsibility. I own it. But I'm out of the cage now and however comforting it looks, however much it seems like a refuge in moments of stress, I'm not going back in. Not for a minute. Taking shelter there with you won't help. Not in the long run.'

Wow. Well, that was a sudden burst of eloquence.

'Nice speech,' I said. 'Mating in captivity. I get it. Now tell me, how long did it take you to write and rehearse that? Did you record it? Practice it in front of the mirror until you were word-perfect?'

She flushed, so I knew I was right. It was a prepared announcement, one she'd had for a while. Something ready to be delivered if she found herself accidentally getting close to me ever.

'We've got more on our plate right now than our love lives,' she said.

She was right, of course. There was more stuff to say, but it wasn't the time.

A couple of hours later and I was driving back North on a more or less empty A1. The occasional lorry. Mist and rain on the road. This ancient highway pre-dates the Roman invasion. How many other people had travelled this way in hope or in fear, fleeing invasion, searching for love or running from it? Going home, leaving home, heading up to burn other peoples' homes to the ground.

I tried hard to find ways to distract myself. The radio helped a bit. Clever people talking. A programme about Britain's industrial past. Another about which contemporary philosophers we might be reading in a hundred years. A thing about business. The regular popping up of the roundabouts helped too. You have to think about the road when a roundabout looms ahead. Change gear. Mirror signal manoeuvre. Change gear again. That always passes a few seconds.

Occasionally I talked to Juliet who dozed on the back seat. I recited to her the names of the villages on the signposts that we passed. Kirk Smeaton, Burton Coggles,

Milton Swanwick. I told her that they could be characters from satirical novels, told her that you could imagine an Evelyn Waugh or a P. G. Wodehouse having fun with those names. She didn't wake up.

She'd been good though. Played her part in getting us through some bleak hours. We left her tied up outside the hospital and at various intervals all of us went and spent time with her, went and walked her around the grounds. She gave us all something to do when the standing around and thinking got too much.

All at once there was the city glowing on the horizon, shining with the spotlit chrome of office blocks, the unblinking geometry of the light from windows in the apartment blocks, the skyline jabbed and poked by cranes. Every Northern city aspires to be like Shanghai these days. Wants to push up and out. Flex some muscle. *This is what a powerhouse looks like, sunshine. Can you cope? Can you handle it?*

Driving on autopilot, I found I'd taken the turning to Stonebeck. The city's grubby underbelly. Its unwashed arsehole. Habit and tiredness combining to pull me towards work rather than home. Told its own story. Told me that I wasn't at home at home. That I was happier at work. As if Selena leaving what was a prison for her turned it into one for me.

Anyway, there was no food at the house. And it was a mess. It definitely needed some of Fiona's from Dusters tender touch. I'd call them-slash-her definitely, but right at that second I was off to Ernies – which was always clean and tidy – I'd make myself a bacon sarnie, hit the bags for a while, drink the emergency vodka, kip on the sofa. Try not to think.

17

MY GRATITUDE JOURNAL

He was wearing surprisingly jaunty paisley pyjamas. Purple and green. A present, I guess. Not something you could imagine him choosing for himself. But maybe he did. He was also wearing some sort of face mask which explained why he brought the faint smell of cucumber with him when he walked into the main dining area of Ernies. Selena used to occasionally indulge in the same sort of thing. Cucumber is meant to be a real boon to the overworked modern skin. I have never moisturised. I suspect that my generation of men was the last to escape the pressure to do that kind of thing.

As he moved slowly, almost daintily, down the stairs I realised that I had reached a stage in my life where almost nothing could surprise me. This revelation itself may, in fact, be the last of the big surprises.

'Hello, Wes,' I said.

'Oh, it's you,' he said.

'Nice PJs,' I said. 'Want a drink?'

'Yeah,' he said. 'Why not?'

And that was bloody well that. Differences patched up. Punch up the bracket put behind us. Forgotten. We'd moved on. We need never talk about it again. Friends. Wes rinsed his face in the kitchen sink, while I rooted out the emergency vodka and the cranberry juice.

Moments later, as we sat at the table in Paperwork Corner, I asked him what he was doing in Ernies in the early hours. He scratched at his chin with fingernails that were, I noticed, nicely manicured.

'Ah. Zoe was pissed off with me because of—'

'Oh, right,' I said, interrupting. 'Say no more.'

He meant that he was in the doghouse because of our little contretemps. Because of the slap the two of us have put behind us and won't ever talk about again. This is the upside of the male approach to aggression, I guess. In the right circumstances a bit of the old ding-dong, a bit of argy-bargy, it can all be breezed over in moments. Put to bed with a handshake and a drink.

'Don't worry, it'll be reet,' he said.

'Yeah, I know,' I said. 'She adores you.'

We clinked glasses. I told him I was putting his wages up. We clinked glasses again.

'Something to put in my gratitude journal,' he said.

'What?'

'Something they got me to start doing inside. Make a list every day of things you've got to be grateful for. Sort of count your blessings thing. Helps keep you sane. Focused on what's good.'

'Accentuates the positive, eliminates the negative?'

'That sort of thing, yeah. Really works. Sometimes anyway. It can make you feel everyone in this country is a lottery winner compared to people in other places.'

Sounded like a good way of keeping people in their place to me. Don't riot on B wing, you're getting three meals a day here and look, there's a complete set of Martina Cole novels in the prison library. It sounded like it was the sort of wheeze those in authority come up with to stop people trying to grab a slice of what the boss class have got. Keep off the grass. Don't touch the exhibits. Don't storm the palaces, don't shoot the princes, think

138

about the fact that you've got Cathedral City extra mature cheddar in the fridge, reflect on the beautiful fact that there are Honey Nut Cheerios in the cupboard, there's a new Netflix crime drama starting tonight and, hey, at least you've got your health.

But I didn't say this.

We sat in silence. Listened to the rain hob-nailing it up on the roof. The wind whipping through the streets like some crazed joyrider trying to outrun the cops.

'Did you ever have to do that thing at school, Wes? That thing where you had to write about how we were going to fill all the leisure hours we'd have in the future. No one was going to have to work much and everyone would have everything they needed so we'd have all these hours to fill. Everyone would be, I don't know, playing golf and learning languages. Making things, inventing things. Going on holiday.'

'No, we didn't do that,' he said.

Of course he didn't. Wes was twenty years younger than me. By the time he was at school everyone knew the idea of the leisure society was such bullshit.

We talked about the kind of world his kid would be coming into. It wouldn't be all flying cars and jetpacks, that was for sure.

What else did we talk about? I'm not telling you. I'm not sure I could anyway. Assume it was football, cars, music and films. The usual. Good night though. The bottle was empty, the next one started and we had apocalyptic hangovers in the morning. So must've been good, right?

We'd kipped down right there in Paperwork Corner under the duvet that Zoe – good girl that she is – had insisted on Wes taking with him even as she was kicking him out of her house for the night. Our feet were warmed by the soft heat of Juliet lying on them.

It was Zoe arriving for work that woke us.

'Well, look at you two lovebirds. What a beautiful couple you make. Should I be worried?' She was smiling though, warming the room with her rare grin. The rain stopped at that exact moment. The wind dropped.

'Now which one of you lazy English bastards is going to get up and make the coffee?' she said.

18

STACKING SHELVES
OR SOMETHING

Ten days later Charlie was brought out of his coma and
moved to a special spinal hospital deep in the Hertford-
shire countryside. Selena, Grace and myself took
rooms in the nearby Travelodge. My dad travelled
down most days. Back North Wes and Zoe ran the café.
Wes was going to kip down in Ernies with Juliet. I
asked Zoe if she was worried about Wes getting into
bother. Zoe told me not to worry, Wes could look after
himself. I should just concentrate on getting Charlie
well again.

Yeah, like it was up to me.

Charlie had to spend a lot of time being prodded at by
doctors, and the rest of us spent our time winding each
other up. Times of crisis are meant to draw people closer
together but it wasn't like that with us. Selena nagged
Grace about university, Grace sulked and sniped at
Selena about Jacob. Selena went on at me about selling
the house and the café. She said she was starting to think
we should probably go with Hobbs, despite him being a
crook.

'Everyone with money is a crook,' I said.

'Well, yes, so we should make sure their wealth gets
spread around.'

'I'll think about it.'

'I know what that means, Luke. It means you *won't* think about it. Not until you have to.'

But she didn't push it.

Bit by bit it became clear that the hospital staff had no idea what the news about Charlie was going to be in the end. The medical jury was out and not coming back in again for some considerable time. No hard news. A lot of head-scratching and chin-stroking. Maybe he would be up and back at rugby training in a few weeks, maybe he'd never walk again. Time would tell. Which was no help. I don't like relying on Time to tell me anything. Time is a slippery sod. Lazy and unpredictable. Plus, Time takes its time.

Nevertheless, it was good news that Charlie was stabilised. He could breathe on his own. He could even talk, if he felt like it – which wasn't often. He could move his arms. He could play shoot 'em up games on his phone. Save the world from the bad men and monsters. Do on screen what no one can do IRL. IRL the bad men and monsters pretty much rule the roost. Meanwhile the police told us that it wasn't likely they'd find out who attacked him. But I wasn't really worried about that. What worried me most was that when Charlie did talk it was mostly about the advantages of suicide. Charlie seemed to have no doubt what the final verdict would be, it would be thumbs down, game over, and he couldn't be jollied out of the idea.

In a voice bleached by fury he told us over and over that his life was finished, that he was dead already, that what was left of him was just a broken ghost tethered to a bed, doomed to look up at the world and everyone in it forever. Sentenced to an eternity of having things done for him and to him. People helping him wash, insufferably cheery orderlies taking him to the toilet. A life of bed baths. Strangers scrubbing his scrotum. How could we leave him to that? How could we be so bloody cruel? Even if he could now wipe his own arse, how could we make him stay in a world where he couldn't do any of the things that really made life worth living? How could we make him live without sport, without even being able to run for a bus? How could we torment him by forcing him to watch ordinary people doing things that suddenly seemed miraculous?

In this new flat, scoured voice he told us he couldn't even watch the telly because there were people on it cooking, shopping and taking their dogs for a walk. Turning lights on and off. Sitting down but also getting up again. Why did we think it was okay to make him have to see all that? His standard refrain was that if he was a horse we'd have shot him by now.

We didn't know what to say. What would you have said? Selena cried, Grace called him names.

My dad meanwhile kind of agreed with Charlie. He tried to make some soothing noises. Chin up, laddo, always darkest before dawn, you'll get through this. But I know my dad. I knew what he was really thinking, what he really wanted to say. Christ, have some dignity, boy. Don't lie around making us all feel bad. Don't make us feel sorry for you. Time to grow up. Be a man about this. Grow some cojones, as Wes might say. And if the news did happen to be the worst thing, if Time finally got around to telling us the bleakest news, then my dad might well be all yes, you're right, Charlie, do us all a favour and check out quietly, discreetly. Earn our respect by slipping away without a fuss.

It's what he would do. What he always tells us he is going to do when the time comes.

Meanwhile I said and did what everyone else did. I cried like Selena, but tried to do it only when I was on my own. I called Charlie names, like Grace – told him to not be such a bloody whinger – but under my breath and only when he was asleep.

I know what this makes me sound like, but you weren't in the room with the boy's howling grief – which was hard enough to bear – or his long seething silences, which were worse.

For hours at a time Charlie simply lay on his bed, face tight with resentment, eyes not moving from the ceiling, willing himself to stop breathing – praying for a heart attack, a respiratory tract infection, a mercifully inexact shot of morphine from a distracted nurse. A pillow pressed over his face by an exasperated member of his own family.

Spend too long in that environment with someone like that and your own mind grows unhinged, you can't trust your own thoughts. They degenerate. They become zombie thoughts, diseased and murderous, stumbling through the night looking for scraps of flesh to feed on.

Aside from us, the most regular visitor was Charlie's mate Joey Viscusi. He was a tall, well-built kid who would be handsome if he didn't look so wretched every time we saw him. We all tried to tell him that it wasn't his fault, that he had nothing to reproach himself for, but Joey wouldn't be comforted. Joey was haunted by the night he and Charlie were attacked. Was thinking of giving up college. Said he just couldn't concentrate any more.

Joey was suffering from a bad case of survivor's guilt. He had only suffered a bruised cheekbone, a black eye and a split lip. He'd had worse injuries playing rugby on an average Saturday.

It was Joey who gave us the first hint that the assault on our kid wasn't random. He told us that he just didn't get it. Told us that you always get nonsense in town on a weekend night, you expect it, but mostly it's juvenile insults and if it does boil over into actual violence it's slaps and scratches. Handbags. Charlie and Joey, they were well equipped to deal with that. Could always give as good as they got, and a bit more actually.

'But this was different, Mr Greenwood.'

'Luke, call me Luke. Different how?'

He thought for a while. 'Because the guys who went for us looked bored, you know? Like it was just a tedious job. It was like they were stacking supermarket shelves or something.' He paused, sniffed, blew his nose into a ragged bit of tissue. 'Sorry, I've had this cold since that night. Drives the girlfriend mad, she says it's psychosomatic.'

'No worries. Here, take this.' I give him a fresh tissue from the packet I always carried around with me then. Not because I had a cold, psychosomatic or otherwise, but because I never knew when I might burst into tears.

'Thanks. Another thing that was weird was that they didn't really pay attention to me. They did just enough to keep me out of things. Few guys whacked me, got me down and held me down on the ground, but it was Charlie they were after. They took their time too. Just laying into him like they were robots and aiming for his back and his head. I've been wondering if he was mixed up in something he shouldn't have been, you know.'

'Like what?'

'I don't know. Drugs maybe. I mean, it was weird the way they were trying to really hurt him. Oh, and the other thing. The most important thing. They were sober. Couldn't smell booze on them at all. They were very controlled.'

'Have you told the police all this?'

'Of course.'

'And they weren't very interested.'

'Not really. I mean, they wrote it all down and everything but . . .' His voice faded away. He asked us what the doctors had said. I told him more than I knew. More than I had a right to. Told him that we were still waiting for test results but that everyone seemed positive. No sense in burdening this nice lad with our fears on top of his own.

'Well, fingers crossed then because Charlie seems . . .' His voice faded again.

Charlie seems. Yeah, he did.

In the end I spent as much time as I could walking Juliet. Selena spent as much time as she could smoking.

You have to find your own path through these things. Whatever works.

19

MIGHT EVEN BE QUITE NICE

One night, Selena and I left Charlie's ward and went and had dinner. We'd been doing this regularly all three of us, a chance to compare notes, discuss strategies or share miracle cures we've discovered on the internet.

This time, however, Grace didn't come. She said she was sick of us. Sick of thinking about her brother, never mind talking about him. She was sick of everything. She had her own life to live. All that.

So Selena and I went to Pizza Hut on our own and we were shy with each other but it was all right. We cried a bit and we laughed a bit and we shared funny stories about the kids when they were growing up.

After a while, we even managed to talk about things other than Charlie and Grace. She didn't mention selling the house or the business and I didn't mention the fact that she ran off with a fuckwit boy half her age and with a quarter of her intelligence. The music was inoffensive and the food was okay, exactly what you'd expect – I'm a closet fan of the bacon bits you get at the salad bar, an underrated culinary delight – and we talked about films and mutual friends. We even looked around the restaurant and tried to imagine the sex lives of the people at the other tables, just like we used to do a lifetime ago when we first started going out.

Before we ordered food Selena had a gin and tonic and I had a beer, and I didn't go on about how a taste for gin is a symptom of a newly nationalistic and non-inclusive Britain. We had wine with the meal. It wasn't great but it was cold and it did what it was meant to. We felt the tension and worry of the last few weeks recede just a little. We needed wine the way paper cuts need Band-Aids. The whole world shrunk to this table in this very two-star diner. It shrank to a size we could manage.

After the meal I paid and we walked back to the Travelodge together. At the door of her room she turned and kissed me on the cheek and said thank you, Luke. And I said, don't worry about it. It was a pleasure.

Then her arms went around me, she pulled me in tight and somehow we were in her room. There's a real mystery to how these things happen. Always a surprise, always magic involved, always a kind of sleight of hand.

Now we were kissing. Now our clothes came off. Piece by piece. The process was inelegant. We ended up hopping between embraces, tugging at our reluctant jeans, my recalcitrant socks. Her rebellious tights. I thought for a moment about the shape I was in. Had Wes's boxing moves and Zoe's diet tips done what they were meant to? Had they shifted some of the chocolate weight? All the worry about Charlie, though – that had to be worth a couple of pounds lost. The grief diet.

I wondered about the little blue pills lying undisturbed in their blister packs back up North. Should I have brought them with me? Should I have known this was going to happen? Been more alive to body language over the stuffed crust and the all-you-can-eat salad? Obviously I was getting no better at decoding this stuff.

'Are you sure this is what you want?' I said, as we fell across the bed. Selena, disengaged from me, sat up on the bed, shrugged herself out of her bra – an everyday one, greyed by a thousand washes, clearly this wasn't a planned seduction. She sat up on the bed, looked down at me for a long cool moment. I couldn't read her expression but I could see that she was in fantastic shape. Maybe she'd never looked better.

I had a sudden picture of Jacob's absurdly beautiful face, him placing the precisely tailored stubble of his chiselled chin between her legs. Though maybe he was still too much of a boy to be enthusiastic about giving oral sex. Nevertheless, a painful image. I was knifed by it. I closed my eyes.

'I think so,' she said. 'It might even be quite nice.'

It was like I'd been punched. I got up. I kept my back to her as I put my pants back on.

Selena sighed behind me. 'Oh, Luke.'

I switched the light on. She blinked in the sudden and unforgiving Travelodge glare as I pulled my sweatshirt on.

'Okay,' she said. 'You're right, was probably a bad idea but how about a cup of tea?' Still I said nothing as I left. Not even goodbye.

It. Might. Even. Be. Quite. Nice.

The cruellest words anyone had ever said to me.

20

BECKHAM OR SIMILAR

Grace and I were heading back up North. We were not talking, we were listening to her playlist. If we talked we'd have to address bad things like Charlie's death wish. We'd have to discuss her failure at uni – why everyone else seemed to be able to go out dancing, drinking, shagging, whatever and still get it together to write a few words about some dead lady novelists. I'm pretty sure that given the chance those dead lady novelists themselves would've managed it. Do we think a hangover would have stopped Emily Brontë? Do we think Charlotte would have blown her loan in six weeks of debauchery or Anne quit at the first sign of a bollocking from the beak? No, we do not.

If we'd talked we might also have had to address the giveaway breeziness between Selena and myself. The way we had chitter-chattered about nothing and absolutely didn't refer to anything that may or may not have occurred between us after our pizza the night before. Selena had absolutely emphatically – and speedily – agreed with my suggestion that if Grace wanted to go home then I should drive her. Yes, yes, she said, it was quite clear that Charlie was feeling overwhelmed with the whole family around his bed all the time. We should go.

If the day had been a normal one, Selena would have been sarcastic – much more *yeah, right, just leave me here to deal with it all on my own, how bloody typical* than the way she was: detached, distracted and more or less silent. Grace must have noticed that our exchanges were even more strained than usual.

So on the way back up the A1 we didn't talk, we just listened to Grace's tunes, almost none of which I knew. Didn't take long before I realised there was a kind of theme, however, a thread running through them. These tracks, the soundtrack to the film of Grace's life, were mostly about forgetting the everyday world and just dancing, getting down on it, getting high. It was several hours of the plot line of 'Girls Just Wanna Have Fun' basically. I could see why Grace and the lady novelists might not have got along. Hard to see where the Brontë sisters intersect with the girls/mindless fun axis.

But I kept my opinions to myself, just kept my eyes on the road as the bald miles rolled by.

I dropped Grace at home, I didn't stick around to hear her pissed-off astonishment at the state the house had got into. I gave her a twenty to buy some food and told her to phone Fiona from Dusters – her card was on the fridge – if she really couldn't stand a wee bit of clutter.

They were pleased to see me at Ernies. Zoe gave me a kiss and a hug. Wes clapped me on the shoulder.

Even more heartening was the reception I got from the punters. The handshakes. The whispered commiserations. Old Ken stood and applauded, but then he's always a bit over the top. Most of the regulars were in: Sad Rosie was there, Chas Diggle, the two Jennies. All of them nodded and smiled. Gave me a thumbs up. Did something to show solidarity. Young Eddard squealed and

151

shook his tablet at me with what seemed like genuine enthusiasm. It was hard to keep from sobbing.

It wasn't just the regulars in either. There were new people too. You wouldn't call it ram-packed exactly but definitely not bad for late afternoon midweek.

Later, just before closing, the customers thinned out and I sat in Paperwork Corner getting the low-down from Zoe. She was all, 'I won't lie, it's been a trying time.'

They'd missed me in the café because it had been busy, but they'd coped. What had been harder to deal with was a campaign of bureaucratic harassment. The almost daily arrival of pest control officers, public health inspectors, fire safety officers, the sudden vigilance of the parking stormtroopers in the environs of Ernies. There had been disruption to water supplies caused by essential maintenance of the pipes.

Every day some new instance of nanny state malevolence. Some grimly inventive jobsworth bullying. Every day a new request to see licenses, every day a new bloke in a shiny Burtons suit requesting a look at the Gas Safety Certificates, the risk assessments, mumbling about the possibility of a full audit.

Just the day before there had been a note that roadworks would start outside the building. The council were, apparently, sorry for the inconvenience but there would be vital and unavoidable hi-vis fuss going on right outside. For how long? God only knew. As long as was necessary.

Zoe told me they'd continued to have problems with youths lurking outside Ernies, and they'd grown bolder. No actual violence but the silent threat of it. The kids older too, leaner, shark-faced rather than shyly ferrety. She thought they might be from outside the area.

Meanwhile the noise of building work bloomed all around us, a spiky sonic thicket grown to put off our footfall. Drills and generators. Ribald shouts of the construction gangs. Gangs that were going somewhere else for their teacakes too.

Then there had been the problems with wholesalers: the deliveries that arrived late or not at all. Several days they'd had to open without milk or bread or bacon. There had also been a noticeable drop-off in the number of hard hats coming in for bacon butties.

'It's definitely an organised thing. The bastards are tightening the screws.'

'It'll get worse too,' said Wes, in his cheery way. 'A lot worse.'

'I thought the place seemed busy,' I said.

'Yeah, we've been getting more local people coming in. They know what's going on and they want to help, but the council contractors have definitely been ordered to stay away.'

'You should have told me,' I said.

'You have had other things on your mind,' Zoe said.

We talked briefly about Charlie. How frustrating his prognosis was, how bleak his mood, how hopeless he felt. Zoe said how it put the trouble in the caff in perspective. Wes said nothing, his face blank. I thought then that maybe he was one of those people oppressed by news of sickness or illness. I got it. I used to be one of those people myself.

Micky Pitts made an appearance just as I was shutting up. As he arrived I realised I'd been expecting him. I didn't invite him in. We stood outside Ernies. His blandly puffy face was loaded with unconvincing concern. He was all like so, so sorry about your son, mate. So, so sad.

'The last thing you need at the moment is to worry about how the business is doing.' He studied my face. He was smirking. He looked like a kid who has found an interesting insect, one whose legs he will pull off in due course. Which is when I knew for certain who had been behind Charlie being beaten up.

There was sudden bile in my mouth. A fist of ice in my guts. I felt my shoulders go rigid.

Micky Pitts didn't seem to notice any change in the atmosphere. He said he was surprised I didn't just accept Tony's offer, to be honest. 'We know it's what your missus wants.'

He paused meaningfully, stepped into my personal space. Looked me straight in the eye, a heavy hand on my shoulder. I could smell his trying-too-hard cologne – *Beckham* or similar. No class. I could see where the skin on his cheeks was starting to pucker and crinkle.

'We're all a bit worried about you. And your family,' he said. 'Worried that things will get too much for you.'

Yes, his pitch was really that crude. The menace that blatant.

He made a stab at a smile. I could see the creeping gingivitis along the gum line. Smell his rank breath beneath the adolescent scent.

After he went, I found myself sitting over an emergency vodka, alternating between extravagant plans for vengeance – the accelerant in his hallway followed by the lighted rag; the snapped brake line in his car; the ricin ordered over the internet and poured in his tea next time he came in. The wild mushroom omelette and, oh my God, how could I have got my foraged fungi so mixed up, Officer? – but I was also thinking how I was so bloody sick of it all. Maybe I *should* just give up. Maybe that would be best for everyone.

I phoned Selena. Told her that I was pretty sure I knew who had attacked Charlie and why.

There was a long silence.

'Selena?'

'Yes. Of *course* it was Hobbs and his bloody minions.'

'Well, what do we do?'

Another silence, then, finally, a slow sigh.

'We don't do anything. We can't do anything. Except sell the business to them.'

'You think we should do that? Really?'

'What's the alternative, Luke?'

I didn't know but I felt sure there had to be one.

When I got home a miracle had taken place in the house. The place shone. Gleamed. Sparkled. Light refracted off surfaces in unexpected ways. Little rainbows everywhere. It smelled of Febreze and fresh air. The windows were open, the heating was off, books and records were back on the shelves. The bins had been emptied and the generalised crud was off the floor.

This was good work, thorough, even by Fiona's standards. Fast, too. They must have had a cancellation. Dusters was normally booked solid for weeks.

Turned out I was wrong about who was responsible for this like I had been wrong about so many things big and small over the last weeks. It wasn't Fiona from Dusters; it was Grace. This was the girl whose room up until she went to university had always resembled a gerbil's cage. A nest of papers and clothes and make-up. A place to hide in. In a reversal of the usual gender stereotypes it was Charlie who was the tidy kid in our house. Of course we thought it was might have been a sign of Asperger's at the time. Every tidy boy has been under the microscope for a spectrum disorder, just as every untidy girl is quizzed about possible friendship issues. *Are you being bullied, darling? Come on, you can tell us, you know. No shame in it.* But truth is, some girls just like to live in squalor just as some boys just like to know where their pens and rulers are, and no one needs to be awarded a disorder because of it.

'I couldn't believe it, Dad. Couldn't let it stay the way it was. Had to do something. Quite enjoyed it actually. Just put some tunes on and got stuck in.' She sounded okay, her voice mild. She told me that she'd made dinner too. Shepherd's pie.

You didn't have to be massively cynical to think that she maybe wanted something.

Grace wanted to talk with me about her future career plans. She turned down the music, which meant her talk was important. She said she wanted to do what I did. She wanted to give university a swerve, escape the debt, wanted to take her chances in the real world.

'You want to be a local journalist?' I said. I was thinking that I might still have the odd contact. Perhaps I could wangle an internship at *The Post* or something.

'God, no,' she said. 'Why would anyone do that? No, I thought I'd work in the café with you.'

'The café your mum wants to me to sell,' I said.

'Another reason you should let me work there. She's not going to let you make me unemployed, is she? I think it's a good plan.'

'Out of the fucking question.'

It was as if I'd slapped her. This was a girl used to us giving in, used to getting her own way with a smile and a cheeky wink, or, if she had to, by stamping her foot a bit. I don't think I'd ever refused her something so flatly. I also don't think I'd ever sworn at her directly like this.

I took a breath. Closed my eyes. Listened to the relentless tessitura that one of Grace's modern soul singers was pouring over some heavy beats. This singer, like all the others I'd heard Grace play, was telling us we have to break free. Urging us to just be ourselves, whatever the cost. To listen to our hearts. Dangerous stuff to be feeding to the nation's youth. I think maybe music like this has a lot to answer for.

I told Grace about the threats to the café, the way pressure was being put on me to give in to gangsters. My determination to resist them. My fear that it was going to get pretty ugly, pretty soon. I didn't tell her that it had already got ugly, that I was sure that this wrangle over Ernies had already got Charlie critically done over and that the police would be no help. She didn't need to know any of that.

'That's brilliant. Means you need me even more. I'll start tomorrow then. I'll come in with you. Help you with "the breakfast rush".'

Yeah, she did the quote thing with her fingers.

'Don't let me oversleep,' she said.

21

MURDERBALL

They were sitting around the bed. As still as a painting. Charlie staring unblinking at a point above their heads. Selena, thin and fidgety, twisting her hands, pulling at her hair. She looked terrible. Like she hadn't slept for weeks. Soft lad, though, bloody Jacob looked all right. Glossy hair flopped just so perfectly over one eye, moisturised skin radiated good health, cultivated stubble gave his face just the right amount of rugged. He could have been an animated Disney prince.

He was lounging on one of those cheap plastic hospital chairs, long legs stretched out in front him, ox-blood Chelsea boots crossed, hands behind his head like he was relaxing on a cruise or something. Like he was in some kind of old style London club. He stood up straight when I walked in though.

'Luke,' he said. He extended his hand. I didn't take it. I didn't even look at him. Instead I looked at Selena.

'Can I have a word?' I said.

Selena sighed, rolled her eyes and shrugged. But she got up and walked to the door I was holding open. Idiot Boy seemed about to say something but Selena shook her head. He sat back down. There's a good boy, I thought.

* * *

In the corridor I asked her straight out. 'Still on with Lover Boy then, is it?'

She pulled herself straight. I realised that I'd done her a massive favour. A minute earlier she'd been oppressed by the weight of gloom in the room, dulled by proximity to Charlie's mute and brooding anguish. Now the adrenalin of irritation at my manner was kicking in and she was coming back to life.

'He's just doing the same as us. He wants to support Charlie. Or, anyway, he wants to support me supporting Charlie. That's okay. I appreciate it. I know he's not my One True Love. Or any of that bollocks. He's unsuitable for so many reasons but, know what? So were you back in the day. You all are.'

'All who?'

'Men. Deeply fucking flawed, the lot of you. You should give Jacob a chance. He's less flawed than most. Smarter than most. And yes, he's young. Too young probably. But know what? Young men are more open-minded, easier to get along with and have fewer hang-ups. At least that's my experience. I know that in a month or a year or five years it will probably finish in some messy way, because nearly everything does and you know what I'll do then? I'll get another boyfriend. Or not, because maybe I won't bother. Oh, what's the bloody point arguing with you? We should be thinking about Charlie right now. Nothing else. He's all that matters. What are you staring at?'

This last sentence was directed at a passing doctor who was looking at us curiously. He stammered off pretty sharpish. Selena turned on her heel and went back into Charlie's room.

That was me told.

I stayed in the corridor for a while, trying to think of things I should have said. I struggle to articulate my thoughts in the middle of an argument. Always have done. I'm too easily overwhelmed by other people's passion. I need time to craft a response. Sometimes quite a lot of time.

I'm sure that with a few more minutes I would have given myself a lot of killer things to say, but the door opened again. Selena. I thought she might be going to apologise. But, no.

'I need a cig,' she said. She pushed past me. I thought about following but there was an energetic militancy about her walk that suggested she was best left alone.

In Charlie's room Jacob was seizing the moment of Selena's departure to tell my son things he didn't have the right to say, things he probably reckoned were hard facts. Things like: couldn't Charlie see what he was doing to his mum? Couldn't he see the hurt he was causing? All that.

Jacob looked to me for support. I kept my face blank. I was thinking, would it make things worse or better if I just twatted him now?

Intent on delivering his home truths, Jacob was oblivious to my growing fury. He stared hard at Charlie lying inert on the bed. Charlie looked like a corpse, only way more sullen. No one has ever been buried looking as grim as he did.

Jacob was persistent, I had to give him that. He started trying to convince the aggressively silent lump in the bed that there could be life after walking and running. That walking and running weren't such big deals in the scheme of things. I paraphrase, but that was the gist of it.

He had an example. There was, Jacob told Charlie, this sport he'd discovered. Murderball. Fast, brutal, like a cross between rugby and banger racing. Beautifully vicious and, as a result of all our dirty little wars over the last twenty years, the UK was brilliant at it. Teams of former soldiers in wheelchairs knocking seven shades of shit out of each other every week all over the country. Something for our Charlie to think about.

'Listen . . .' I began, but Charlie stopped me.

'No, Dad, let him carry on. It's inspirational stuff this. Tell me more, Jacob.' His voice was ominously calm. I may not be great on subtext, but even I could detect the dangerous edge in his voice. Jacob flashed me a nervous smile in my direction. Nervous, but smug. You sap, I thought.

Since the first moment after Charlie came round from his coma, the staff at the hospital had been trying to find ways to cheer him up, to make him think that life still held possibilities for him. There had been daily, sometimes twice daily, visits from various spiritual guides attached to the hospital. The C of E guy, the Catholic guy, the non-conformist ladies, the Buddhists, the Sikh guy and the woman from the Humanists – they'd all been in multiple times. He'd had a dozen leaflets, innumerable invitations to attend support groups both online and In Real Life. He'd ignored them all.

The religious guys weren't up to it anyway. They all melted under his withering and enraged silence, the atmosphere de-oxygenated by our boy's implacable rage. They came far less often now anyway. The nurses too had become irritated as their professional chirpiness ran up against the hard wall of Charlie's bitterness, like insects hitting double-glazing. A hedgerow bird flying into a windscreen. Left them dazed and cross, wanting to start fights. Who needs that in their life?

Jacob was leaning close to Charlie's bed now as he talked, a hand actually on the covers as he continued to talk Murderball. Speaking fast he explained the rules: its

USP as a Paralympic sport. He'd read an article: 'Each player is given a score based on the severity of their injuries, with 0.5 the worst and 3.5 the best you're allowed. Whole team of four players isn't allowed a score more than eight. They call it Wheelchair Rugby officially. I thought—' He broke off as the door opened and Selena came back into the room, bringing the smell of rain, fresh grass and tobacco with her. She carried a paper bag.

'Cakes,' she said. 'From the canteen.'

There was a silence in the room. Somewhere outside there was a siren. A dog barking. A kid crying. These are sounds you can hear anywhere in England and at any time.

From the bed, a grunting laugh. 'Mum, how come you managed to hook up with such a total cock?'

I looked at Selena's face as she flushed.

Charlie had pulled himself up now, his face also flushed as he laid into Jacob, as he gave him a proper verbal hammering. As he told him that if he thought a bloody game was going to take the place of the use of his legs then he was a fucking imbecile. A fucking retard.

His mum tried to calm him down. 'Charlie, love—'

Then the miracle.

Jacob stood up. 'Hey, you kicked me. I felt it through the covers.'

'Are you surprised?' I said

'No, Dad, you don't get it.' Charlie's voice was hushed. 'I *kicked* him. And I meant to do it. I moved my own fucking leg.'

Those spiritual gurus shouldn't have worried, shouldn't have been so easily discouraged: saints come at weird times and in odd shapes, as they should have known.

This hospital was once a country house and so while the doctors and nurses gathered around Charlie's bed to cluck excitedly over this unexpected development, Selena, Jacob and I sat together in what used to be a drawing room, a place for genteel ladies to receive suitors.

I imagine it was once decorated with oil paintings of ancestors or the stuffed and mounted heads of stags. A room furnished with leather armchairs. Couches. Day beds for those eligible ladies to lounge on, whereas now it is just used by dazed and dysfunctional family members of patients. People sipping at too hot brown drinks. The almost-coffee, the not-quite-tea. The cakes that taste of plastic.

Spookily, it seemed Jacob was also thinking about cakes. He launched into a rambling monologue about how he couldn't understand why hospital shops sold food that kills you. He said that maybe I should bid for hospital franchises.

Stupid sod, I thought. 'Thing is, Jake, old bean, Ernies also sells food that kills. Sugar, salt, saturated fats . . . You can't survive in the catering business unless you worship that particular holy trinity, certainly not in Stonebeck. Yes, every forkful takes you closer to a diabetic future of amputated extremities, but that's the way people like it.'

'Oh, right,' he said.

Oh, right, indeed.

But I found I didn't have the energy to hate him any more, especially not since it was his ridiculous chuntering on that had sparked a major breakthrough for our kid. So I just agreed that it was weird that food that murders the consumer should have to be served in bags designed to protect the environment, and after a while he lapsed into silence.

If there ever had been portraits in that room they had been replaced by hectoring posters urging us to take better care of ourselves. To think about doing more exercise. To give up smoking, drinking, living. Similarly,

163

the stags had been swapped for prints of inoffensive geometric abstract art. You know the kind: Rothko-lite. Meaningless but soothing.

Easy listening music played softly. Or the music that has somehow become easy listening. It was cutting-edge contemporary pop once. Glen Campbell, Neil Diamond, Joan Armatrading. 'Wichita Lineman', 'Sweet Caroline', 'Love and Affection' – songs I already loved but would love more now that they were the soundtrack to my kid's return to life.

Funny, the journey from edginess to respectability. I guess one day the same will happen to the music of my own generation. In thirty years, in this room or one very like it, people will be saying: come along, Grandad, time for your Sex Pistols, time for your Stiff Little Fingers. You know how you love a bit of punk before your nap.

I didn't say this. If it had only been Selena there with me maybe I would have – it was the sort of thing she might have found interesting once – but this Selena, the With-Jacob Selena, this was someone I didn't really know.

After a while she leaned over and touched my face.

'I'm sorry,' she said. 'I really am.'

22

A JOINT APPROACH

Large parts of Stonebeck were walled off now, the area's reconstructive surgery being hidden by grey metal walls like the ones you see in countries undergoing civil war, and by wooden billboards shouting RISING ABOVE THE EVERYDAY TO CREATE ENVIRONMENTS PEOPLE ENJOY and BUILDING THE FUTURE IS OUR GREATEST ADVENTURE. Plus artists' impressions of a generic modern city. Happy consumers in a glittering wonderland of glass-walled retail opportunities.

Meanwhile we were still suffering from the loitering yobs looming into the personal space of the punters, the steady drip drip drip of fatiguing legal letters from the city council and the continuing deluge of one-star reviews on Chip pinging fake outrage about milky tea and serving-wench backchat almost hourly.

The reviews appeared from a variety of names and locations, and they were shared across all platforms. Some tweenage intern at *The Post* picked up on it and wrote a story without even coming to me for a quote. It ended up as a splash, even though there was a city-centre car-jacking to report that day.

I could deal with all this though, could tough it all out. I was beyond caring about all that. I could also deal with the news – broken to me by the same intern – that the large American coffee chains were circling locations in Stonebeck like the sharks they were. Won't this be the death of Ernies? he asked. The final farty squeeze of the plastic ketchup bottle of our existence? How did I feel about that?

The answer was not much because *my feelings* were mostly taken up by being pissed off with my children and their little betrayals.

There was, for example, the phone call from Charlie that began well but deteriorated until it ended very badly. Charlie wanted to apologise for putting us all through the ringer, wanted to tell me that he appreciated the support now that he felt things were obviously getting better. I told him not to worry about it, it was all understandable, that he'd actually been a lot more stoic than I'd be in the same circumstances.

But he had other things to say too. Things that were harder to hear.

'Dad, I've had a lot of time to think.' A long pause. 'And you need to know I reckon Mum was right to leave.'

He didn't pause for breath after that but launched into how his injuries had put things into perspective, made him realise that if you think you want to do something you should just do it. He told me how maybe Selena and I had got in a rut. Said he could see how things had got unbearably routine for his mother, my wife.

'I think you probably had both got too comfortable. You needed something dramatic. New challenges sort of thing.'

I hung up on him.

Meanwhile, at Ernies, his sister gave me some of the same grief. They'd obviously been talking about it, developing a joint approach.

'Come on, Dad. You were the one who said we were being too hard on Mum, said we should cut her some

166

slack, and you were right. People shouldn't have to stay with their partners if they're miserable. When something's dead you bury it and move on. Me and Charlie, we were just being emotional. Suppose we felt like Mum was denying our childhoods, like we'd been living a lie growing up, but I know that's all a crock. It's like when I tried to hang on to my toys and you wanted to jumble sale them. Remember the barney we had about that? Things just stop working sometimes and you just have to chuck them out, however attached you are to them. Everything breaks eventually. Toys, cars, phones, relationships, everything. It's best to realise that and just deal with it, you know?'

So there you are. Life according to Grace. Marriages are like phones. They break.

The contract runs out. You get an upgrade.

I couldn't help feeling we'd somehow failed as parents.

'Anyway, you wouldn't want me to stay with some boring bloke just because I was married to him. If it was me going out of my mind with boredom you'd be telling me to leave, to come home, that there was always a place for me at yours.'

You want to know how I reacted to that? The mature example I set? I sent her home. Told her to hang up her apron and go. And yes, she sighed. Yes, she rolled her eyes. Of course she did.

'See you at back at the ranch,' she said.

Was that really the conclusion Grace had come to? That I was just another boring bloke? That her mum had been repressed? The lesson here is that we should never find out what those closest to us really think about us. We might never recover. Anyway, I'm not too sure that I would say the things she thinks I would if she was in a dull relationship. I might be like my own dad. I might be saying that all long-term relationships have their sticky patches, their stagnant pools. Sometimes, you just keep wading on, knowing that there's firmer ground and decent views ahead. Sometimes, to use her own metaphor, you don't just get a new phone. Even if you drop it down the toilet you fish it out, wipe it, put it in a bowl of dry rice and wait. Often, miraculously, you find it starts working again.

A couple of days later I spoke to Selena, who was very cheery. She told me that she'd had a long chat with Charlie where he had expanded on what he'd said to me, that he even gave her a list of places to go when she and Jacob finally do get to go travelling.

'How's that going?' I said

'It's fragile at the moment,' she said. 'I'd really appreciate it if you didn't screw it up for me.'

'Tell me, what can I say or do that will screw it up? Give me a hint,' I said.

She laughed, but there was a wobble in her voice. She was nervous. 'I'm not telling you that, or you'd just go and do it, wouldn't you?'

I heard her inhale. She was smoking. I pictured her flicking ash on to the ground, pacing. Pulling at her hair. 'Don't you worry, Luke. It'll almost certainly end in tears.'

'Can't wait,' I said.

There was a pause then. Seemed like I was expected to say something, to offer something. An olive branch.

'Oh, by the way, I'm going to sell Ernies,' I said.

It was that simple in the end. I opened my mouth and that was what came out. Completely unplanned and a surprise even to me. Especially to me. Ridiculous. Imagine if Churchill had risen in Parliament back in June 1940 intending to give it the full We Shall Fight Them On The Beaches and had instead found himself saying that we were running up the white flag and that he for one would be signing up for German lessons.

Still, I can't pretend it wasn't a relief, the thought that I could just stop now. That's the paradox of surrender, I guess, that it brings liberation. There's joy in giving up. In letting the waves close over your head.

23

I ATE HUMMUS AS A CHILD

I was the last to get to The Swan. I was as keen as anyone to start drinking but first I wanted some time on my own to think, so I invented an errand and wandered for a while in the drizzle. The stiff cold breeze lifted the plastic bags and sent them swirling up to the second-storey windows, where there were no steel grills, almost as if they were alive and looking for a way out of the weather themselves. I kicked a discarded polystyrene cup and tried to avoid the dog shit.

If I squinted in this rain I could imagine the surge of another century's mill workers. Could imagine being jostled by the ghosts of men and women exhausted from fourteen-hour shifts, some of them missing fingers from a slip at the loom. Making their way home dreaming of fried fish, cheap booze and sex, the perennial comforts of the poor. Could imagine the bootless urchins looking for dock leaves to take home for dinner.

In the real world there were no workers left, just the bench-drinkers working their way through the plastic torpedoes of cider. Their silos of bliss. They looked like they were having a lovely time. If you've got to be in a male-only group, a crowd of alkies is the best place to be. Your bench-drinkers might mildly hassle you for change, but they don't lurch through the streets thinking they're

God's gift. They're okay. They are blokes who have found a way to stop the world and get off, who have found a way out from under all that job, bills, direct debits, children, qualifications nonsense. A way of dialling down the bloody relentless noise of everything. Things are simple. Q: Do you have a drink? A: Yes. Conclusion: you're fine. And if the answer happens to be no, well, then you now have a goal. Something to aim for. You have direction.

Selena and I have travelled to a lot of places. We have taken our perfect summer beach reads to all-inclusive resorts in Portugal, Greece, France, Turkey and Tunisia. We have stroked our chins in front of holocaust museums in Berlin, Tel Aviv and Warsaw. We have hiked pilgrim routes in Andalucia. We have visited ancient battlefields in Scotland and newish battlefields in Croatia. We have shaken our heads at what passes for art these days in New York and Bilbao. We have been to Centre Parcs dozens of times, played swingball in Blackpool and Camber Sands. We have had theatre breaks in London and spent time glamping at Latitude and Green Man. We once flew to Helsinki just to see Leonard Cohen in concert. Yes, we have been reasonably imaginative when it comes to taking holidays, yet every time it came to decide on a destination for our annual fortnight away I thought that it might be nice to take a couple of weeks to live like an alcoholic.

You wouldn't want to do it all the time – it seems like a tough gig as a full-time occupation. It's more a vocation than a job, demands sacrifices in the way that being an athlete or a writer does. You can kiss goodbye to a family life for a start – but as a break, it might be okay – especially if the weather was sunny.

I decided then and there that once the ink was dry on the contract, once the money was in my account, I'd have a gap year of my own down here with these guys.

I imagined myself sitting in shy silence on the edge of the group for a few days, before someone sidled over and asked me for a cig. I'd have a packet ready, bought for just that moment and then we'd start chatting and I'd share my tinnies and that would be that. I would be in. Part of the group.

It would be like when I changed primary schools in 1967 and let Malcolm Roberts have a go on my yo-yo, or like when I joined the badminton club a few years back and loaned Pete Gill my favourite shuttlecock. It's how it always is in male communities. A period of solitude and then the lads approach, circle round you, sniff at your arse in a metaphorical way and then ask you to prove you're an okay geezer by some small gift or some small act of service. You do that and you're in. Probably the same everywhere: in the Vatican as in Morris dancing groups.

And when the Gap Year was over? Well, who knows? It might turn out to be a vocation after all.

So I ordered a pint and watched my little group of employees from the bar. My soon-to-be ex-employees. The pub was as quiet as ever. The other customers were as few in number and as immobile as ever. But around the table Team Earnshaws had commandeered there was animation. Life. Zoe was telling a story, her gestures fluid, loose, acrobatic almost. Her features sharp in that over-lit space. Grace sat leaning forward, lips parted, smiling, and her eyes never leaving Zoe's face. They had really struck up a rapport.

Zoe had been suspicious of Grace working at the café. Had rolled her eyes at the idea of the boss finding a job for his daughter, disgusted that nepotism seemed to be everywhere, in cafes as much as it was in big business, in media, in politics. Brazen discrimination in favour of the boss class was everywhere and it made her sick. Maybe I should have told her I'd been against it too, but had been steamrollered by Grace. Anyway, despite her reservations, they had quickly formed a good team. They made each other laugh, and Zoe had seemed to enjoy taking on a sort of mentorship role.

Whatever the story Zoe was telling now I think Wes had heard it before. He had the sort of detached smile that suggested a man with a mind elsewhere. He was relaxed though, content to let Zoe perform. He liked watching her shine.

I reached the table just as Zoe's tale reached its climax. From the little bit of it I caught it was another boys-and-their-incomprehensible-ways story. Zoe has a lot of these. Grace and Wes laughed, but I had the sense that they would have laughed louder and for longer if I hadn't been there. I felt a rush of panic, sweat under my arms. If I'd been driving it would have been another of those times when I'd have had to pull off the road until the sense of futility subsided, would have had to close my eyes until my awareness that everything dies – is dying right now – had passed.

It was then I told them of my decision to sell Ernies.

There was a moment of quiet. No one said anything or did anything for a minute, then Zoe put her hand on my arm and that was all it took. I found I was weeping like a child.

'Oh, Dad,' murmured Grace, while Wes went to get me a whisky, and Zoe, the most practical, produced a more or less clean tissue from somewhere.

No one tried to talk me out of it. I had wondered if they might. Wondered if I might have to reassure them that they had prospects, places to go on to once the café was turned into luxury mews apartments or whatever. All of them had significant barriers to gaining future employment after all.

173

On the surface Zoe was the most employable. She radiated competence, but being pregnant would count against her obviously, despite the laws saying it shouldn't. What would count against her even more than this was her inability to take shit from morons. Her glaring inability to keep her lip buttoned. But if she could bring herself to put on the right professional face and gear she could get work, could nab herself a proper job with rights, possibly even a pension. She could always teach if she absolutely had to. Use her various degrees even. In Hungary if they didn't let her stay here.

Wes might struggle though, might come up on somebody's computer database as a person with breach of trust issues. And Grace was a university drop-out with no experience of anything much and no discernible work ethic. She'd also expressed an interest in taking the place over at some point in the future so you'd expect she might be a bit put out by my decision to quit, but no.

Zoe was the most vocal in saying what a good idea it was, how it was definitely the right time for me get out and get on. To make some positive changes. She seemed determined to keep her chin up, to see this as something to celebrate.

'Change is always good,' she said and insisted in getting a bottle of bubbly. Real champagne. The bartender was a bit shocked. It's fair to say that The Swan is not your typical champagne establishment. I was surprised they even had any but he told us that it was actually good stuff. Moët & Chandon. Properly chilled, properly aged.

'We've had it in the cellar for years,' he said. 'Old landlord bought a crate in 1990. He was expecting England to win the World Cup. We always have a bottle in the fridge in case something momentous happens. Birth of a princess, something like that.'

174

Like a lot of places that have been kept poor for centuries, Stonebeck is weirdly monarchist. Bunting appears as if by magic for every royal occasion. No royal is too minor that their engagements can't be celebrated with a street party.

Two glasses in and Zoe was really warming to her theme, and her theme seemed to be what a liability I had been to my own business. What a fuck-up I was. She didn't say it but it's what she meant. I was too tired and too depressed to argue. Champagne is meant to cheer us up, but in my experience it does the opposite, takes a good mood and slices it into petty arguments, slow-to-leave migraines and roiling guts.

'Yeah, you *should* sell up,' she was saying for something like the fortieth time. 'You don't even like running the café. You lack passion.'

Years ago Zoe had come across an article about why cafes fail. Lack of passion was number one ahead of poor position, poor service and poor pricing. It had made us laugh at the time, the very idea of being passionate about serving breakfasts.

She told me now that I couldn't cook, couldn't chat to the customers and couldn't do the bookkeeping. Couldn't do the basics.

'What Dad is good at,' said Grace, woozily, 'is delegating. He finds decent people to do the stuff he doesn't want to do.'

'Yeah, you are probably right,' I said. See, too fatigued to argue. Anyway, I wasn't thinking about the café. I was thinking about all the things I'd been no good at, all the things I'd given up or delegated. Pretty much everything. Work, love, life. I wondered now if I had even somehow delegated care of my wife to Jacob. Conjured him up to do the things I could no longer be bothered with. Right then it seemed possible.

175

I noticed – eventually – that the table had fallen silent. I made an effort to be a sport, to join in.

'I don't feel great about delegating Ernies to the likes of Tony bloody Hobbs though.'

I saw Zoe and Wes exchange a look. *Now?* her face seemed to be saying. *Yes, now,* his seemed to be saying back. They did this a lot these days, this talking in glances. It's a useful skill.

Zoe took a breath. 'You *shouldn't* delegate old Ernies to their care. I – we – have a better idea. You should leave it to me, to us.' She gestured to herself and to Wes.

She was rehearsed. Had clearly been preparing for this moment. She told me she had a business plan and more than this she had money, savings. She blushed slightly as she admitted to the shame of having access to even more cash if she needed it. A good line of credit.

'Bank of Grandma.' She laughed as she took in our gobsmacked faces. 'We have that in Hungary too. I never said I was poor. I'm an immigrant not a beggar. Totally bourgeois, me. I went to Tuscany on holiday growing up. I ate hummus as a child.'

People are never quite what you think and almost never how they present themselves. All of us our own inventions.

'How much are you offering?'

She named a figure. It was less than half what Tony Hobbs would pay. Definitely not silly money.

I thought about it for a full half-minute. Thought about all the trouble that selling the café to Zoe would cause. Thought about the danger it could put everyone in.

The others were looking at me wondering what I would say. To be honest, I was wondering that myself. I couldn't be certain of anything any more.

'Okay,' I said.

176

'Really?' She seemed astounded. Her mouth dropped open comically. I laughed for what felt like the first time in ages. Something else occurred to me then.

'Yes, really. Or sort of. That figures gets you Selena's share, plus one per cent, enough to buy her out and put you in charge. And, luckily for you, I happen to know that your new business partner – the new owner of the remaining 49 per cent share – will be amenable to you taking over and running things.' I turned to Grace. 'That's you, by the way. I'm going to give you my share.'

Grace was grinning now too and I realised, with a pang, that I hadn't seen her smile like this since before her A level exams. We hadn't done a lot of a lot of smiling in our little family for some time. None of us.

Wes stood up, tall and lean in his loose white shirt and jeans. He had new shoes, I noticed. Campers. He'd looked a lot more put together since being with Zoe. His whole look was stronger.

He called across the pub to the barman. 'Hey, Stevo, we're going to need some more of that fine fizz. Fact,' he says, 'break out the crate. We'll all have a glass.' He gestured to the whole pub. The living dead shifted in their seats. One or two raised a slow glass in thanks. Truly a day of days for them.

Later I asked how Zoe was going to deal with Tony Hobbs and with the council, with the proposed redevelopment of the café. As I said this, I realised it was maybe a conversation we should have had earlier.

'Don't worry,' she said. 'I've thought about that. It'll be fine. We've got a couple of things on our side. Your daughter's come up with a scheme actually. We've got it all worked out.'

For the last hour I'd been chatting films and music with Wes, while Grace and Zoe had been gossiping and giggling together like kids. I'd been vaguely wondering what it was they'd been talking about.

'I should just tell him that Ernies is not for sale to him. That it will never be for sale to him. That he should just accept that.'

'Don't do that. Not yet anyway. It'll cause more trouble before we're ready to deal with it. I'm hoping that in the end he'll just give up of his own accord.'

'What if he doesn't?'

'I think he will. We've got a plan and we've got something on our side that is 100 per cent reliable. Something you can always count on.'

'Oh, yes? What's that?' said Wes.

'Male vanity!' Zoe and Grace said this together – shouted it almost – and they laughed because of this. They embraced and then high-fived. Zoe spat fizzy wine across the table.

'Great minds,' said Zoe. She wiped her mouth with the back of her hand, dug out a paper hankie to mop the table.

The girls looked so young, so happy, so full of life that I felt a chill. I glanced at Wes. He was frowning and I knew that he felt it too.

24

A WORD

'Virgin's piss, mate. I can't drink that.'

Micky Pitts was in Ernies watching me pour the almost colourless tea. It was true, I had gone too early with it. Nerves, I guess.

'It's hot and it's wet and you're not paying for it,' I snapped. 'It'll have to do.'

Nevertheless, I stopped pouring, replaced the big brown pot on the table to let it brew some more. I saw Pitts's eyes roam the café. They lingered on Grace as she wiped a table near the window. She had her back to us. She was wearing tight black jeans, not really suitable for a long shift in a café. I thought I'd maybe get Zoe to have a word.

'Now there's something I'd like to see hot and wet,' Pitts said, and laughed unpleasantly. 'Where did you find her? She's bloody gorgeous.'

I was about to tell him that she was my daughter when Grace turned round and caught him staring. He looked away. I thought he might even be colouring slightly. She just shook her head, turned back to the table. I imagined her smiling to herself. Imagined her expression. It would be amused and faintly baffled all the same time. *Oh, men, why are you all so feeble?* Something like that.

* * *

Micky Pitts was here to repeat Tony Hobbs's offer one last time and, if I still didn't seem inclined to accept it, to threaten me with yet another escalation in the campaign against the business: the full legs have been known to break, cafes have been known to spontaneously combust. Children of recalcitrant proprietors have been known to end up paralysed. All that.

It was this knowledge of why he was there that meant I stopped myself revealing that Grace was my daughter. She'd be a whole lot safer if Pitts and his boss thought she was just a random waitress.

'Look,' I began. I stopped.

'Yes?' said Micky, his voice mild. His tongue did a snaky little flicker out of his lips. 'I'm gasping here, mate. Shall I be Mother?' He picked up the teapot. I took a long breath.

I wanted to cut to the chase, to get this over with. Whatever Zoe had said, whatever her plan was, I felt I should just tell him that that he was wasting his time and that he should just drink his tea and go. That he should tell the puppet-master that can't you win 'em all, that the pickings from the Stonebeck redevelopment were going to be rich enough without our little bit, God knows.

It wouldn't do any good saying this, of course. People like Hobbs, people who like to see themselves as winners, they don't think like that. They take any thwarting of their desires as a kind of assault, an injury, something that cuts right at their sense of who they are. A wound that must be avenged before it can heal. That's the difference between narcissists and the rest of us.

Anyway, I didn't get to deliver my spiel because Grace materialised at our table. I noticed that her red Ernies T-shirt seemed to be a size too small. Pitts looked her up and down. Yes, Zoe should definitely have a word. As soon as.

'Can I get you gentleman anything else?' she said. 'A buttered scone, perhaps?'

There was this sort of playful light in her eyes. I didn't like it.

'Stop it,' said Pitts. 'You're getting me all hot and bothered.' So predictable. So lame. He went on to say that – regrettably – he'd have to decline the scone. He had to watch the old figure. He did a little paradiddle on his belly with his fingers.

'Oh, and I should warn you, love, there are no gentleman at this table. Are there, Lukey, old mate?' he said

I didn't say anything. What could I say?

'That's okay. I'm not mad keen on gentlemen anyway.' Grace gave the word 'gentlemen' just a touch of emphasis.

Pitts pushed his chair back from the table. It scraped on the floor. He lounged back, his chest expanded, he spread his legs. He grinned.

'Not mad keen, eh? Now is that because you're keener on the ladies, like,' he jabbed a thumb over his shoulder towards where the two Jennies sat, 'or is it because you like men but ones who ain't gentle.'

She gave him a frank, appraising stare. Answered his question by not answering it.

'So I can't tempt you to anything? Anything at all?'

'Oh, you can tempt me all right, darling.'

I know. This was the standard of the dialogue. At this point in the twenty-first century. Painful.

That's another thing to ban when I am CEO of the UK. Thick middle-aged men doing flirtatious banter. Should be punishable by serious jail time.

Micky Pitts kept his hungry eyes on her as she sashayed all the way back to the kitchen. She took her time too. Knew the effect she was having. Something else Zoe could have a word about.

I was a bit disappointed in Grace, to be honest. Up to now she'd been professional, hard-working, a quick learner. She'd been an asset to the team, but she seemed to be in a funny mood today. Not herself.

'Fuck me, she's a minx, your new waitress. Saucy as hell. Definitely up for it. You're going to have trouble there, mate. She's going to be driving the old geezers crazy.'

'Just say what you've been sent to say, Micky,' I said.

He finally poured that tea. It was a rich soupy brown. 'You already know what I'm here to say, Lukey. Don't you?'

'Yeah, I do.'

'So all I can do is urge you to be sensible. Tony's patience is wearing very thin. You know, I think I will have a scone after all.'

He headed up to the counter and I watched as he had another little exchange there with Grace. I wondered where Zoe was. I hoped this wasn't going to be the way things were in the future, Zoe taking things easy. Sitting on her arse while Grace did all the work. Dealt with all the reptiles. I was thinking that it was maybe that Zoe felt she'd done her time taking that crap. Seemed almost like she'd decided to take her maternity leave early anyway, she'd hardly been around at all the last few days.

Grace and Pitts were too far away for me to hear what they were saying. The radio, the rattle and clank of cutlery and crockery, the hum of the punters' talk, it all meant that their conversation didn't carry, however hard I tried to tune into it. I could see the body language though. Lots of teeth. Lots of eye contact held just a little too long. Pitts leaning on the counter in a way that suggested both familiarity and ownership. Their hands touched as she passed him a plate with a scone.

When he came back to the table I noticed that she had given him way more whipped cream than we usually allowed customers. Wanton acts of largesse of this sort eat into the tight margins of any well-run café business. I added this to my list of things to tell Zoe to have a word with Grace about. I wondered idly if maybe I could suggest that we introduce a formal Performance Management procedure with employee targets and development plans and all the stuff that Selena used to talk about of an evening.

'Very glad I popped in here today, Lukey. Very glad.' Pitts took a big forkful of scone. 'Only thing that would mean my trip had gone absolutely perfect would be if you could tell me that you were going to say yes to Tony.'

I looked at his big, ruddy face with its rumours of collapse making themselves known around his cheeks and under his eyes. I watched as he chewed. That careless chomping with big square teeth. There was cream at the corners of his mouth. Jam on his chin.

'Can't do that, Pittsy-boy,' I said. His eyes bulged. *Pittsy-boy*. It's done his head in. 'No can do.'

Yep. *Pittsy-boy. No can do*. I actually said that. Did the job. Enraged the man. Result. Past a certain point tiny victories are the only kind you can hope for.

25

LONDON ROAD

Grace was going out. She was a bit secretive about it. Said it was just a night out with the girls and then batted away any further questions by calling me Victorian Dad and suggesting, quietly and firmly, that I just butt the fuck out.

'I'm a big girl, Dad,' she said.

But she wasn't really. Still isn't. We parents, all of us everywhere, we agree on this. At some level our children stay small and tender-skinned forever.

When she finally emerged from the bathroom claiming that she was ready to go she looked . . . well, she looked unsubtle, let's put it like that. The first thing you noticed was the hair, and the hair was actually okay. Glossy as the coat of a well-fed Afghan hound and dropped in ringlets like you might see on some stately home portrait of a restoration duke. Some real libertine. It was sort of amazing actually. A work of art.

Yes, the hair was fine – but the rest of her . . . Shoulders bare, midriff bare, legs bare. Leopard print skirt hardly more than a belt. High-heeled sandals revealing toes painted a neon pink. Full warpaint. Skin everywhere. Cleavage, probably the result of some wardrobe engineering. Her collar bones on display and looking as fragile as the legs of a hedgerow bird.

This was a whole new get-up for Grace. She looked like one of the girls we occasionally gave free tea to after they'd had a hard day's night giving blow jobs in a variety of dull cars and vans. I was distressed by it, to be honest.

She didn't ask me how she looked. This was just as well because an honest answer would have caused a row. I don't think I'd have been able to avoid sounding like a victim-blaming high court judge in a sexual assault case. Say nothing, I told myself. Really. Say nothing, Luke. Nothing.

I said something. 'You'll catch your death.'

Grace smiled briefly and put on a – very bad – Southern American accent as she paraphrased Dolly Parton: 'Do you know how much money it takes to look this cheap?'

'Yeah, most of a student loan,' I said.

Her mouth twisted. 'Funny guy,' she said. She tottered forward on those ludicrous heels and hugged me so hard the breath was almost squeezed out of me. She rumpled my hair.

'Love you, Dad,' she said. Then, 'Oh, bloody hell, you're not going to cry, are you?'

It was true that I was welling up. 'Just be careful.'

She looked at me oddly. 'I always am.'

A taxi did a nagging honk. She moved towards it carefully. On those heels she was like a newborn giraffe not yet in control of her limbs. I wondered what her brother would say if he could see her now, deliberately making walking hard for herself.

I took the dog for a run, a long one. I ran along the London Road. Maybe it's not surprising that the longest street in every English town and city is the one called London Road, but do they need to be such shitty streets? Every London Road I've ever seen has been a grubby ribbon of traffic crawling past ugly houses, Brewers Fayre pubs, and filling stations. A series of small parades of shops. Each with a bookies, a hairdressers, a newsagents. All of them looking like they're about to close forever.

The fact it was drive time didn't help. The gleam of LED headlights through steady rain made this road look like the set of some dystopian feature film aimed at adolescents. Easy to imagine zombies haunting these parts of the city. Cost-cutting by the council meant half as many street lamps as there used to be a few years back, and those that were left had these new bulbs that seemed to give out half as much light as the old ones did. When the city council was not handing over the city to private speculators, it was busy investing in gloom.

It was hard going. There was a stabbing pain in my back just beneath my shoulder blade, an odd sensation in my lower gut, my left eye felt twitchy and I had a mouth ulcer coming. My legs were heavy. Juliet kept up with me easily, and she's a lazy dog. All of these things made me think of cancer. I was at that age after all. Jogging painfully into sniper alley. Reaching that zone where you could be taken out at any time. Heart attacks, embolisms, aneurysms. The age where it was still a surprise that our bodies let us down. But not very much of one.

It shouldn't be any kind of shock really. By fifty-eight we all have a lot of dead friends after all. By fifty-eight we've already been to too many funerals.

I struggled to overtake mothers with baby strollers. Pensioners gave me concerned glances as I wheezed past them. Most worrying thing? Teenagers not giving me lip. Fact, they also looked a bit worried, as if they feared this gasping wreck lurching towards them pre-figured the kind of apocalyptic horror show they spent so much time scaring themselves about. It was like they were anxious in case I collapsed at their feet and did something embarrassingly adult like die in front of them while begging for the CPR which they didn't know how to do.

Whatever, their forbearance told me that I must have looked almost as bad as I felt. The teens were anxious about me. Could there be anything more humiliating?

I made it home alive somehow. I tried to decompress. I opened a beer, I ran a bath, I played uplifting music loud. The Undertones. Nothing worked. Nothing did what it should. I was oppressed by a feeling that everything was wrong, that nothing had quite the shape it was supposed to have.

In the bath I drifted into a kind of waking dream, befuddled by heat and bath gel. Watermelon and Cumin. For the man that thinks a little differently. A special offer. Did I think a bit differently? Was I watermelon and cumin worthy? Maybe I was once, but now? I'm really couldn't say any more.

The whole time something was bugging me about Grace: the way she was dressed, her nervousness, that unexpected last hug. It wasn't just a desire to impress a lad. There was something else going on. *She ruffled my hair, for God's sake.*

I had always been able to tell when Grace was up to something. No big deal. I'm claiming no special powers: all parents know when then their kids are in trouble. It's a sense you develop pretty damn quickly, the ability to spot a child over their heads, out of their depth, trying to get away with stuff. You might sometimes ignore the messages you get via this parental radar – sometimes ignoring them might even be the best thing to do – but you can't ever pretend that you didn't know something was wrong.

After my bath I phoned her. She didn't pick up. I didn't leave a message. No point – a fact of modern life is that no one ever listens to a voicemail. I texted her. *Call me x.* Then I phoned again. And repeated the process. I was assuming she'd eventually be forced to think there was an emergency – something to do with Charlie maybe, a relapse – and she'd have to answer. Took a while, but worked in the end.

'Dad, this had better be important.'

'It is.'

'Well?'

'I'm worried about you.'

'Jesus.'

'Where are you?'

'In a bar.'

'Which bar?'

'Just a bar. It's quite tacky, but it's definitely not dangerous. I'm fine.'

I didn't say anything for a while. I was trying to listen to the ambient noise. Trying to work out the background music. Twangy, trembly, wobbly guitars.

'Dad?'

'I'm still here.'

'Can I go now?'

'You're really not going to tell me this boy's name? Or where you're meeting him?'

'No.'

'So there is a boy.'

'Well done, Sherlock Holmes.'

'What time you'll be home?'

'I don't know. Late.'

'Okay.'

'Okay?'

'Okay.'

I heard her exhale slowly. Her voice dropped to a whisper but it also softened.

'Dad, I appreciate the concern. I really do. I really am fine. If things stop being fine – if I even think that there's

188

the slightest chance they will stop being fine – I'll call you.'

'Thanks. All I ask.'

'Bye, Dad. Love you.'

'Bye, Grace.'

I was happier now. Not because of her reassurances, but because I knew where she was – that background music something of a giveaway – and because I was going to take myself down there and hang about outside, until closing time if I had to. And then I was going to insist on giving her a lift home.

I had only been going to read and listen to music anyway and I could do that as well in the Audi as anywhere else. So, cheered up, I hit the kitchen for snacks to take with me. I made a thermos of hot tea.

26

SNAPS

I was sitting in the Audi with the radio on half-listening to a programme about early female playwrights – more of them than you'd think and all bawdier than the men – and skim-reading Steig Larsson – plenty of inspiration there for people like me who found themselves playing private eye. I was completely prepared for the fact that nothing would happen, that I'd be here for an hour or two, treating my car as a sort of cosy mobile living room, before Grace emerged.

Worn out from the run, Juliet snored gently in the back seat.

Do you know the Tahiti Hideaway? According to a recent piece in *The Post* it's a city institution and a fun place for a first date. It's the bar in the old railway workers' social club behind the station. It's a deliberately Yorkshire take on Polynesian island culture. Swaying plastic palm trees, swishing grass skirts, flaming zombie cocktails in coconut half shells. But at the same time you can always get a pint of Tetley's with a decent head on it. Pork scratchings. Based on the music I had heard in the background, it was there that Grace and her mysterious beau had gone.

The door to the bar opened. Light tumbled out into the damp night like a drunk being ejected. A man and a woman were briefly silhouetted as they stumbled past the bouncers. They were wrapped around each other. It was, for just a few seconds, like a scene from a stage musical. I couldn't hear it but I imagined they were laughing, giggling. They had the sloppy body language of people finding themselves hilarious. The man swung his partner round into his arms and they kissed briefly.

That partner was – of course – Grace. The man? It was – of course – Micky Pitts. I realised as I saw him that this was somehow what I had been expecting all along. Another example of the routine clairvoyance of parents.

What to do? Here was the bloke that had almost certainly led the crew that almost crippled my son, and now he had his butcher's hands all over my teenage daughter. What would an ordinary person do? Something violent probably. Something vicious. Something anyway. Run the car at the guy maybe. No one would blame them. No jury would convict.

The door to the Tahiti swung shut as Pitts moved in on Grace again and the acid orange light spilling from the lobby was abruptly cut off. A few seconds of blackness and then a series of flashes. Each one illuminating our smooching couple. Someone was taking pictures. I got a whole series of tableaux, tiny glimpses of startled faces pulling apart from one another.

A sudden memory of an incident I'd long forgotten swam back to me. Me catching Grace snogging a boyfriend on the doorstep after a night at some gig or club or party, me adopting a voice of high mock-pomposity. *If you must osculate in that manner then can you kindly do it away from the house?* Grace giving me a cheerful one-fingered salute without even breaking the snog.

The photographer was Zoe. Of course it was. Zoe as a balletic paparazzo ghost-dancing around her targets. A wildlife photographer capturing the death of a wilde-beest at some waterhole.

I had been transfixed up to then, pinned to my leather-ette seat by surprise, but now Juliet barked and it was like a starting gun firing. Finally I was out of the Audi and moving fast towards this crazy street-theatre, the insane pavement panto my daughter was caught up in. I still didn't know what I would do, but I would do some-thing. Then Pitts let out a shout, murderous and terrible. I broke into a sprint. Juliet gasping behind me. Illuminated with another flash I could see that Grace was clamped to Micky Pitts's ear with her teeth.

Micky was swearing and trying to throw her off. He crouched suddenly, and Grace went over his shoulder. Landing on her back with a thud that I felt in my guts. I felt sick. She coughed. Tried to raise her head, flopped back, which is when Pitts placed his foot very deliber-ately on her neck.

I noticed his heavy work boots. Road-mending boots, almost certainly steel toe-capped. I thought, in the random way we think these things: who wears steel toe-capped work boots on a date?

Zoe had stopped taking photos. Her phone was out of sight and we were standing next to one another, the other side of Grace's prone body, facing Pitts. The door of the club opened again, chucking its fresh light onto the pave-ment. A bald and goateed bouncer poked his head out. I felt momentary relief. It was quickly stubbed out.

'You all right, Micky?' said the bouncer.

'Yeah, fine, mate. No worries.' His voice was steady.

'Okay, then.'

The bouncer withdrew his head. The light was chopped off again. He had seen what was going on and realised that it was time to choose a side, and he hadn't chosen ours.

Silence now. Or more or less. Near enough. There was traffic, of course. Muffled announcements from the station. Would Inspector Sands make his way to the concourse. Sirens. Bass-heavy dance music from a car stereo somewhere. More music from inside the club. Men shouting. All of it adding up to a soundtrack so familiar it might as well have been silence.

Pitts looked at us, wiped his nose and mouth with the back of his hand. He was breathing heavily. A man out of shape. He pushed a hand through his hair and moved his foot very deliberately backwards and forwards on Grace's neck. She whimpered. Unfurled her legs.

I felt relief. She was alive. She could still move.

Zoe and I looked at each other, uncertain. Fear put its palm against us. Held us in place. Kept us where we were. This wasn't our territory and Pitts knew it. He gave us a snaky smirk. Licked his lips.

Grace lay on the ground, very still again now. I noticed a cigarette packet next to her head, picture of a diseased mouth. She was making drowning noises deep in her throat. Sounds that were choked from between clenched teeth. She coughed out a gobbet of something. A strangely neat and circular package of blood and phlegm. I could see a hard nugget in the midst of it. A tooth. She coughed again, more blood, more mucus. She made feeble movements with her legs and arms. Like a distressed fledgling bird fallen from a nest. That boot on her neck. One quick stamp. All it would take.

'Hush, love, hush up, please.' Pitts's voice was intimate somehow, almost tender.

Grace did what he said. Pitts shifted his foot for better purchase. He was going to do it, I was sure of it.

'I'll have that phone.' His hand was outstretched. 'Quick.'

I looked at Zoe. She didn't move.

'Just do it, Zoe,' I said.

'Yes, Zoe, be a good little girl and throw it over,' Pitts said. He put on a silly voice. Stretched out the syllables of her name. He was like a middle school kid trying to act hard now – *yes, Zo-eee. Throw the phone, Zo-eeee* – I was thinking that I could rush him. I could do him. I had fast hands.

But I didn't move. The wind caught the cigarette packet, trundled it down the street.

There were a few more moments of stillness before Zoe lobbed him the mobile. Pitts made no attempt to catch it. He picked it up from the ground, slipped it into his pocket. He moved his foot from Grace's neck, dropped to his haunches, crouched over her.

'Leave her alone!' My voice was raw. Embarrassingly high-pitched too.

The words echoed off the cobbles and the warehouses. Juliet snapped and snarled. Pitts ignored us, same as the old streets did. Nothing happened. No one came running. There was no help. There was just us and the rain. I took a step forward. He looked up. I stopped.

He smiled as he looked at my dog. 'And you can piss off,' he said. Juliet slunk behind my legs. Pitts laughed, a little mirthless bark of his own, then turned his attention back to Grace.

'Come on, love,' he said to her, his voice quiet again, tender again. He helped her up. 'You'll be okay. I just don't know why you had to be so stupid.' He shook his head. He sounded genuinely upset. A headmaster let down by a favourite student. Like he'd caught the head-girl smoking weed behind the bike sheds when she should have been at choir practice.

She made it to her feet wincing. She was barefoot now, the stupid heels kicked off. She was holding the elbow of her left arm with a cupped right hand. I'd

194

watched enough rugby matches over the years to know what this meant. A broken collarbone. People do it instinctively, holding the elbow helps with the pain from a shattered clavicle. There was blood running from her nose and a ragged black hole where a front tooth should have been. She stuck her tongue in the space, getting used to the new shape of her mouth. She tried to hide it behind her hand.

'I thought we were getting on. Having a laugh, weren't we?' He still sounded betrayed somehow. He straightened up, became businesslike again. 'I strongly suggest that you accept Tony's bloody offer for the café now because I'm telling you, fucking gloves are off.'

None of us said anything. He turned and walked into the dark. There was an exaggerated cowboyish swagger to the way he moved. It was weirdly camp. Zoe went to Grace. They clung to each other, Zoe murmuring, sort of crooning almost. Wordless comfort. Juliet tried to nudge her way between them. If there were cuddles going, she wanted her share.

As they pulled apart, I noticed jerky activity. Zoe's thumbs were dancing on the keypad of her phone. Her phone.

'What are you doing?' I said.

'Sending a few interesting snaps to Tony Hobbs.' She said it matter-of-factly, the way that on another day she would say that we'd run out of beans and someone had better get down the cash-and-carry. 'Got some nice ones where he's got his tongue right down your daughter's throat.'

'Was like a fat lizard. Like having a psychotic frog in my mouth,' said Grace. Her voice was flat, but she didn't seem upset particularly. Sounded tired more than anything.

'Well, you know what they say. You have to kiss a lot of frogs before you find a prince.'

Zoe's thumbs were still working her phone.

I began to speak. I wanted to ask how she could send photos when she'd given her phone to Pitts? As ever, she was ahead of me. 'Here's a pro tip, Luke – always keep a shitty phone that you can hand over to bastard thieves while you keep your real one safely hidden. There. Sent. All done.'

This then had been the plan. The thing that used male vanity against itself. A plan I should have guessed. A simple honey trap. Blackmail. Pitts's ego means he thinks the pretty girl really likes him. You get him into a compromising position. You take photos. You threaten to expose him to his wife and her vengeful family if he doesn't get his father-in-law to call off his pursuit of the caff. It's the sort of thing that could only be dreamed up by women who think that all men are idiots. Girls who think that the future world – the one where young women run everything – is already here, when in fact there's probably a generation or two of fighting still to be done.

The old geezers, the ancient silverbacks, the self-proclaimed leaders of the pack, they don't hand anything over with a smile and a shrug. Not money. Not power. They are as mad as hell, facing the end of the world and determined not to take it all lying down. Sad really. Things are often a helluva lot easier when you do take them lying down.

I closed my eyes. Lifted my face so I could feel the wet rain on my face. There has been rain most of the days of my life. If I moved away would I come to miss it? There was the sound of cheesy dance-floor classics leaking from the Tahiti. Boney M. 'Ma Baker'. The smell of the canal. A boy-racer growling away from nearby traffic lights in a pimped-up city car. A Mini maybe, or an old Fiesta. It would be something like that.

'Zoe, isn't the thing with blackmail that once you actually expose your target then your leverage goes?'

She snorted. 'Leverage. Anyway, let's just see what happens.'

Silence again. Grace came over to put her arms around me. She was shivering. She felt so thin.

'Hey, Dad, it'll be okay,' she said. 'Thanks for coming. I appreciate it.'

She scratched Juliet's ears. 'You can tell you were once in the police,' she said to her. 'Never getting stuck in when you're really needed.' Juliet wagged her tail happily.

'How did you get Hobbs's number?' I said to Zoe.

'Everyone is contactable,' she said. 'Everyone.'

'There's an app,' said Grace breezily. 'And you know what, Dad? I think I probably need to go to A & E.'

'And, mate, you should see an emergency dentist,' Zoe said.

Grace gave her a gory, blood-framed smile.

'Dad?' she said.

'What?'

'No need to tell Mum about all this.'

I didn't argue.

27

WE ALL WANT TO BE REMEMBERED

'Trouble is, there's no ordinary decent criminals any more. No one you can rely on.'

Hobbs was inviting me to think about the strange decline of the United Kingdom. Think of the things Britain used to lead the world in, he said. Manufacturing, design, mining, engineering, retail, film, even music. Outsourced now, all of it. The mines have gone and the factories are following them, the household names of the High Street only exist in the fading memories of those who can remember a pre-digital age. All the surviving brands owned by foreign multi-nationals.

It was just after ten, the breakfast rush was over and Tony Hobbs was having poached eggs on wholegrain toast. Wes hated making poached eggs, they so rarely came up to his perfectionist standards. I wondered if Hobbs knew this. It wouldn't surprise me. No power trip too small for a proper narcissist.

'Think of the ordinary decent criminal things we used to be good at, Luke.' He ticked them off on his fingers. 'Extortion, thieving, fencing. They're all gone now too. Or they've got much nastier. The Krays and the Richardsons went and no replacements came through. It's like football: we invented it and now we're shit at it and we're shit at crime too. It's all just about the money now. The heart's gone out of it. Crime is all about drugs now, like football is all about money. Spoilt things.'

His point was that the Artful Dodger is dead and Fagin is in a witness protection programme. The crime world he knew is all just archive footage on the History Channel now.

'The last of the old-school British gangster crews are probably the IRA and the UDA,' Tony said. 'And they don't really count, being Micks.' Then he was off on one about the way the new style underworld bosses dressed. How the decline was very evident there. 'These days everyone dresses like bleeding salesmen. Off-the-peg suits from Burtons. Easy to iron shirts.' His lip curled in disgust.

Well, yes, I thought. Gangsters would rather be sales execs. Of course they would. Criminality is a bit of a mug's game. Drugs, extortion, thieving, violence – the hours are long, the pay much worse than they expected and the working conditions are rubbish. Your colleagues are bastards and pension provision is non-existent. Sentencing is getting much harsher. And no one in their right mind wants to spend more than twenty-four hours in a UK jail. It's just not safe. No one is that reckless, certainly not any halfway intelligent criminal.

'You can't get the staff,' I said.

'Not from Britain you can't. We've lost the spark.' Hobbs sounded genuinely regretful.

It was pretty quiet in Ernies at the time. There was the music, of course. Something bleepy that I didn't recognise. Grace had taken over the choosing of the sounds. I'd been expecting complaints from the regulars but there had been none so far.

Hobbs finished his breakfast, put his knife and fork together neatly. Wiped his mouth with a napkin. A fastidious man.

'I should thank you really,' he said. 'Or thank Zoe and your daughter.' He nodded towards the counter where the girls were chatting. There was a lot of nodding, I noticed. A lot of wrinkled brows and serious hand gestures. I knew what they were talking about. Menus. They were obsessed. They talked about café stuff the whole time. Sometimes they talked about marketing and promotion, sometimes about the launch. Sometimes they bickered good-naturedly about whether or not they should keep the name Ernies and if they did change it then to what? M words are current favourites: Muse, Mooch, Mighty Fine. All very modern, none of them right.

'I've been wanting to get rid of Micky for years,' Tony said, his tone reflective. 'A shame it had to be this way, but, you know, he knew the rules. Joanie's a bit upset. But she'll get over it. Once she saw the photos she knew there was no going back. She did really love him, you know.' He shook his grizzled head at the strangeness of it, at how bloody weird people were.

'We don't die of love,' I said.

Hobbs looked at me sharply. 'People die of love all the time, Luke. The lack of it anyway. Biggest killer there is. Alcoholism, obesity, suicide, drugs. They're mostly all diseases of the heart. No, I'm just glad they never had kids. Would have been a trickier thing then.'

'Where is Micky?' I said.

'You won't see him again.'

'Yeah, but where—'

'You're not a journalist now, Luke. You don't need to keep asking questions. He's gone, he won't bother you again. Man was a disgrace.' Past tense. Worth thinking about. 'And, by the way, you know I never sanctioned the assault on your lad. That was Micky's own initiative. I'd told him before about the dangers of thinking for himself. Had always strongly discouraged it.'

He poured tea. It was the colour of seasoned mahogany. Proper builders. 'Thing is . . .' He looked up at me and smiled. Those teeth. 'Thing is, Luke, I still want the café. Sorry, but there it is.' He made it sound like this wanting was an illness, something he couldn't control.

'We've got a problem then,' I said.

Tony sighed. 'I get it, Luke. I do. You've built something and you want that recognised. We all want to be remembered. I know I do.'

He stopped there. Looked around him. He seemed uncertain about how to progress for a moment. He took a deliberate breath, swallowed and ploughed on.

'So I was thinking, one of the new streets . . .' He paused again. Sat back. Spread his arms. A beneficent emperor dispensing a gift to a peasant. 'How about Luke Greenwood Street?'

I laughed. Daft.

Hobbs laughed too. Didn't sound like he thought anything was funny though.

'Doesn't have to be street. Could be Luke Greenwood Square, Luke Greenwood Avenue, Luke Greenwood Place. Could be Luke Greenwood Palace Gardens, for all I care. We could put a blue plaque up if you want. You know, "On this site stood Earnshaws: widely recognised as the finest café in the world". I don't care. Whatever it takes. Within reason.'

Mental. Hobbs was still smiling, but he was also studying my face carefully. Possibly wondering if I was the kind who might choose to push the boundaries of what within reason meant.

'I could also find jobs for your staff, you know. I need people, we've already established that. Zoe, Grace, Wes – between them they demonstrate an impressive range of skills. Or I could set them up in a new café somewhere else. London Road maybe. I have interests there. Lots of possibilities.'

'I thought you wanted ordinary decent criminals.'

'I also said those days were over. I'm totally legit now. More or less.'

Sad Rosie got up and shuffled over to the counter to settle up. The old till rang.

'Another angel gets his wings. Hey, maybe old Tony is less of a fuck-up in the afterlife.' Hobbs chortled.

Was that a confession? Pretty ambiguous if so and very deniable, I suppose. Anyway, businessmen-slash-gangsters are total self-aggrandising bullshitters, all of them. A confession is hardly solid proof.

Another bell. The café door this time.

'Another angel,' Hobbs began. He stopped, he looked stricken.

I turned. I was half-expecting Pitts to be there, re-appearing from whatever mincer he'd been fed through. From whatever happy pigs he'd been thrown to.

Of course it wasn't Pitts. It was Margaret, Tony's wife. You could tell at a glance that she was on a mission. She stalked into the cafe with the stiff determination of a goose with goslings to protect. She was on alert, ready for battle. She came over to our table.

I stood up. 'Thanks for coming,' I said.

'I had to come. Don't worry, love. We'll get all this sorted.'

Felt nice to be called love like this. Found myself welling up.

Margaret sat down and picked up a menu but didn't look at it. Instead she took a long, slow look around the café. It seemed to be more or less what she expected. She picked up one of our big plastic tomato-shaped ketchup bottles. 'Very retro,' she said. She put it back down.

I was pleased to see the table was pretty clean. For some reason Margaret's approval was important to me.

She had things to say. She began by reminding Tony that he'd been promising to retire for at least ten years, that he wasn't very well, that she thought it might be nice if they could have just a little peace before Time's winged patrol car finally caught up with them. Hobbs didn't argue. Just sat and listened. Then she poured a second cup and explained, as if to a child, that he should remember that she knew everything about his business. That she knew where all the bodies were buried.

'She's speaking metaphorically of course,' said old Tony. He glanced at me. The menacing bonhomie had vanished. He was flopped in his chair like he was wounded somehow. The calm authority was all gone, replaced by unattractive blustering. He was red-faced and twitchy, pulling at his collar as if his shirt was too tight.

I felt for him. A bit. A tiny bit.

Margaret said nothing. Maybe, her silence said. Maybe not. Besides, she had something even more damning in her armoury.

'I have all the admin,' she said. 'I kept proper records.'

She had also brought admin with her. She had a contract all drawn up and ready for signing. A piece of paper in elegant legalese where Hobbs swore he wouldn't attempt to undermine the café.

I didn't think we'd need it. It was very clear that Hobbs was no match for his missus. That he wouldn't dare take her on. That he knew if he did, he'd lose.

I wondered why I hadn't thought to call her before. It had – of course – been Zoe's idea to do so now, and I wish she'd had it sooner. What had taken us weeks of sweating and agony to try and fail to resolve was sorted by this woman in the time it took to drink two cups of green tea.

In under half an hour it was all agreed: Tony was retired, Ernies was saved and today was the first day of the rest of our lives. Gap years all round.

I should send Margaret round to speak to Selena. The UN should send her to knock heads together in the Middle East.

'You said it,' she told me when Hobbs was in the toilet. 'You said it's our time now. Women like me. We can have the world if we want it. Just took me a while to wake up to it. To shake off the chains.'

'To break out of the cage.'

'Exactly.'

I didn't tell her that I was just paraphrasing something my wife had said to me after she'd left me. We didn't need to dwell on that.

'Why do you stay with him?' I wasn't being provocative. I was genuinely curious.

She looked at me like I was mad. 'Because I love him. Because I knew what he was into when I married him and,' she took another sip of tea, 'because he really hasn't got long anyway.'

Turned out Hobbs was a very sick man, that he seemed to have most of the degenerative diseases a man can possibly get – Alzheimer's, Parkinson's, vascular dementia, cancers of the prostate, the kidney, the liver, even the bloody ankle. Mostly at an early stage, to be fair, but still.

'I didn't even know you could get cancer in the ankle.'

'You can get it anywhere.'

She told me that she thought it was this pile-up of his various conditions that had prompted the sudden determination to be the founding father of Southside. She thought it was his last hurrah.

'Raging against the dying of the light,' I said.

'Exactly,' she said. 'And if you ask me, a man raging against the dying of the light is the most dangerous kind of man.'

When Hobbs came back he said, 'I bet she's told you, hasn't she?'

'Told me what?'

'That I'm riddled.'

Riddled. Such a good word. Only ever used about two things: cancer and woodworm.

'She has, yeah.' I looked down at the table, didn't want to meet his eyes. Didn't want to see a being-brave face.

'It's okay. I've had a good innings,' he said. He shuffled into his seat. I looked at him then. He blew his nose. He looked at the ceiling. I followed his gaze. It needed painting. When did I last have it done? Not recently. Not this decade anyway.

'Regrets, I've had a few,' he said.

'But then again, too few to mention.' I was trying to jolly him along. Trying to not let him feel he'd been humiliated just because he'd been out-manoeuvred by women. By his *wife*, for Chrissake.

He didn't answer. I looked at him. He was crying. He was bloody crying. Tears making their tentative way over the crevices and the crags of that dying face. And, of course, that set me off. So there we were, two blokes sitting at a table in a greasy spoon in Stonebeck, one middle-aged, one older, and both of us weeping like orphans over the things we'd lost. That's the thing people don't get. Or, if they get they just don't talk about. Men are leaky bags of salty water. All liquid. All tears.

'Bloody hell,' said Margaret. 'Zoe, love, can we have some tissues over here?'

28

LUNCH IS NOT FOR LOVERS

Which brings us to now. Launch night at the new look Earnshaws. I'm pleased they've kept the name, though I'm not sure why, given that it was Darius Peretsky's choice of name and nothing to do with me. Zoe tells me it was because otherwise Wes would insist their baby was called Ernie.

'He's a sentimental old sausage sometimes,' she says. She loves all these English terms of endearment. Old sausage, Piggy-wig, me duck, Pog. The things the English call their loved ones, they tickle her.

The new management have changed everything else, which ought to irritate me but doesn't somehow. Place needed a facelift. Menu has been streamlined too. It's all about the Hungarian stews now. Apart from the breakfasts, the entire menu consists of a few basic dishes. Goulash of course but also Csirkepaprikás, and Halászlé with Főzelék for the veggies. They've all been road-tested and have gone down surprisingly well with our clientele. The regulars have even quite enjoyed learning how to pronounce them. People in the café slur away like it's a Sean Connery convention. *Cshirkerpaprikash, Halarhshzelay.*

Dr Zoe has a theory. Of course she has. 'Britain is a country in need of comfort right now and Hungarians are the best at comfort food. We just are. It's what we do. We've had so much sorrow in our history, and food is the way we've learned to heal the heart. Food and sex. Those are things Hungarians are very good at. Things we can teach you.'

'I'll take your word for it,' I said.

It's a practical change too. A good stew is healthy fast food basically: prepare it in advance, keep it hot on the ring and ladle it into rusticky bowls the moment the customer asks for it. Add a hunk of bread (50p extra) and job's a good un. Makes life a lot easier for the staff. No more waiting at tables for a start.

The fluorescent lighting has gone. The décor now is moodily spartan. Farmyard browns, industrial greys. Lamplight. Imagine the works canteen of a firm of anarchist poets. This is fitting because under the reign of Zoe and Grace Ernies will be way more than just a place to eat and meet. It'll be a gallery and a pop-up theatre. A venue for spoken word and nu-folk gigs. Cabaret. It will be a hub of creativity. A free university basically. There'll be foreign language lessons in the evening. There'll be indie film nights. Philosophy and discussion groups led by Zoe as she puts that doctorate to good use at last.

Outlining her business plan a few weeks back Zoe had said that it was her goal to make Ernies the go-to spot for those vital one-woman shows about mental health issues.

Before I could say anything Grace had jumped in. 'She's joking, Dad. And Zoe can make those kinds of jokes. You can't.'

Zoe had just laughed, had said that actually she wasn't joking and gone on to say that Ernies would also be a centre for political campaigns, especially those against gentrification.

There were, I felt, things to say about this, things about possible ironies and paradoxes, but not my place to mention it. Instead I'd just told them it all sounded great.

I look around me now. There is Jacob, there is Selena. They can't keep their eyes off each other. Or their hands. Look at them for any length of time and you see pinkie fingers entwined, hands brushing invisible flecks of dust off shoulders – arses patted, arms stroked. They look like kids in love. So weird.

It's okay. They are off next week and we'll see the damage that too much holiday can do to a relationship. When she wants to see some of the local culture and he just wants to sit by the pool; when she wants to read her book and he wants to talk bollocks or get shit-faced or both. When he gets the runs in Morocco or they can't get Wi-Fi in Peru. When he eyes up the waitress in Hong Kong. When she pisses him off by phoning one of her children every day. When they realise that the world is big but Airbnbs are small. When they are faced with each other all day every day.

Holiday intimacy is like disease, redundancy and old age. Not for sissies. There's a decent chance that they'll hate each other by the time they get back. Which will be good news, obviously. I haven't gone completely soft.

Charlie is there, standing. Out of hospital especially for the occasion. Every day he can do a bit more. Walk a little further. Doctors are excited about his progress. He is in what used to be Paperwork Corner talking to a pretty young woman who I vaguely recognise. I wander over.

'Hey, Dad, you remember Gina?' he said.

I do. I remember a rabbit of a girl with panicked eyes. I remember a generalised wash of pale distress at Charlie's refusal to do anything to help himself in that Buckingham hospital. Her frustrated hurt at his determination to die at a time of his choosing. She was one of the nurses there.

She is transformed now. As transformed as Charlie himself, in a way. Her gaze is direct, she laughs easily, slugs Punk IPA from the bottle as she tells us that she's got to get out of the healing people business to do something more creative.

I hear this sort of thing all the time. It makes me wonder if there is anyone who actually likes what they do, anyone who wants to carry on doing more of it?

'Maybe I'll turn up at one of the open-mic sessions here, tell some stories of hospital life. You see everything there,' she says. She winks at Charlie.

Not often you see a girl wink. I like it.

The regulars are there: the two Jennies are giddy because young Eddard's baseline assessment suggests he might be a gifted child. They put it down to the wide range of interests he's encouraged to explore via his tablet.

Chas Diggle regales some mournful hipsters about great gigs he's seen. Tells them that the only consolation of being an old git is that you got to see all the cool bands. The Clash, The Jam, X-Ray Spex. One of the hipsters makes the mistake of confessing ignorance of X-Ray Spex. Poor sod. He's in for a long night.

Sad Rosie arrives hand in hand with Ken. And, actually, she's no longer in the least bit sad.

Later I get to talk to Ken about this. It isn't the first thing we talk about. No, first we have to discuss the fact that the bowls of Central European solace the Ernies team are giving out beat anything ever served up when I was in charge.

'Ken, you only ever had toast anyway.'

'That's because anything else might have killed me.'

'You do know it's still Wes cooking, don't you?'

'Yes, but now he's got proper line management checking what he's doing.'

I give up. This is when I ask him about Not-Sad Rosie.

'I've been in love for her for years,' he says simply. 'It's why I kept coming in. Just to see her. I was too shy to say anything of course. I've never been too good with the ladies.'

'So what changed?'

He gestures towards the door. I follow his gaze: Steph Baber, Rosie's TV writer friend disengaging from a taxi. There is a jolt in my chest. *Oh Christ. Here we go.* I had thought I was immune to this sort of stuff.

I have to concentrate hard to keep my eyes on Ken as he tells me how Rosie had told Steph that she had feelings for Ken, but couldn't say. Said that she liked the way he clowned around, liked the way he dressed.

'Steph found out where I lived and came and told me that I'd be an idiot if I didn't ask Rosie out. Made me call her there and then. I don't mind telling you I was bricking it. It was like being fourteen again. Couldn't believe it when she said yes, nearly wet myself. We went to the Tahiti Hideaway. Have you been there?'

'Yes, I've been.'

A sudden image of a man's boot on a girl's neck, a memory of the sound of that girl hitting the street hard. A broken tooth sitting on the pavement in a jus of blood and saliva. I think about what might have happened to that man.

Not that I'm mourning him any. Some bleeding-heart 'Thought for the Day' artiste would probably say that every death diminishes us, but I don't think they'd be right. Some deaths diminish us a lot and some hardly at all. Anyway, for all Hobbs's sly humble-bragging Micky Pitts is probably still alive, ducking and diving incompetently down south somewhere. Like the poor, violent fuck-ups are always with us.

'We didn't like it,' says Ken. 'We went back to Rosie's place, spent the night making up our own cocktail recipes and, you know, one thing led to another. I'm a very lucky man, Luke.'

I look over at Rosie, she is smiling as she hugs her friend.

Ken grins as he follows my gaze. 'Oh, and you know Steph is also single, don't you?'

'How would I know that, Ken?'

The party is almost over before I get the chance to talk properly to Grace. Her eyes glitter, her face shines. She smells of beer and sweat. She is quite drunk.

'Dad, you made all this happen. Thank you!'

'Wasn't really all me. Other people played their parts,' I say.

She laughs, mouth wide. They've done a good job on her teeth, you'd never know she'd had one of her front ones kicked out just a little while back.

'What are you like?' she says now.

'What do you mean?'

'Can't take criticism, can't take praise. You need help, Dad. Therapy. Big time.'

I change the subject. 'Nice to see that nurse here with Charlie. Chance of serious romance, do you think?'

Grace pulls away from me. She holds me by the shoulders while she examines my face. She's tall, I think. I'd never realised. Somehow she had grown as tall as me without me really noticing. Her gaze is vaguely off-centre. Her smile falls away for a moment, then returns wider than ever. She seems to make an important decision. She pulls me into another hug.

'I love you, Dad. I even love the way you somehow get everything wrong.'

211

Which is when she tells me that there is definitely a chance of romance. But not for Charlie. Not tonight anyway. 'Gina's not a nurse. She's a doctor, a consultant actually, and she's here because I asked her,' she says.

My face frames the questions. That journalistic who, what, where, when. Grace grins again.

'You remember the night when you went to dinner with Mum and I stayed back at the Travelodge?'

'I remember.'

'Of course you do. Well, I didn't stay back at the Travelodge. I went out with Gina and—' She stops, she even blushes a bit.

'And cocktails. One thing led to another,' I say.

'Yeah. More or less,' she says. Her eyes are dancing. 'Why do you think I had that playlist on in the car?'

I remember – all those exuberant dance-floor hymns to female emancipation.

I close my eyes. I remember the night before that too. Her mother and me, the fumbling with jeans, the inelegant clinches, skin sliding on skin, her telling me that sex might even be quite nice. I feel foolish now. It *would* have been quite nice. And quite nice is okay sometimes. Sometimes it is all you want. Sometimes quite nice is absolutely all you need.

'You're not shocked, are you?' Grace is frowning, pulling at a stray strand of hair in the way that her mother does.

'No, Grace, no, I'm not shocked. Gina seems very lovely. Are you going to be all right looking after Juliet while I'm away?'

Grace laughs at this blatant subject change, this all-too-obvious attempt at swerving around any more talk about my daughter's love life.

'Yes, Dad. I'll be fine with Juliet.'

* * *

I catch up with Selena and Jacob just as they are leaving. The mother of my children and I air-kiss awkwardly. Jacob and I shake hands.

'Selena, if you need anything, anything at all, you can call me any time.'

'She won't,' Jacob begins.

'Shush, Jacob,' she says, flapping a hand him at dismissively. I almost feel sorry for him. Almost.

'Thanks, Luke, appreciate it,' Selena says. 'I can't imagine needing any help but good to know you're there, that you're looking out for me. Same goes for you too of course. Anything, any time, I'll even come out if it's really necessary. All the way to Gallup, New Mexico or Amarillo or wherever – when are you off?'

'Day after tomorrow.'

'So you're really going to do it. Route 66, all of it?'

'Chicago to LA. More than 2,000 miles all the way. I'm going to be my own road movie. Sunglasses on – moving from diner to diner, motel to motel.'

'Sounds awesome, and you're really going on your own?'

'Yeah, just me and a rented vintage Cadillac. Country music on the eight-track cartridge.'

I don't tell her that I might just hang out for a year on the park benches drinking cider instead. I'm still thinking that might be an interesting thing to do. I'll see how I feel in the morning.

We hug. Not so awkward now. She's ditched the new scent, I notice. She smells of herself: of fruit, of biscuits. She softens against me. Yes, quite nice. It definitely would have been quite nice.

Then they're gone, her and Jacob, arms wrapped around each other, stumbling a little like they are in a three-legged race in a junior school sports day.

I think about my trip. Huge stateside breakfasts, eggs over-easy, pancakes and syrup. Grits – whatever

213

the hell they are. I think about how I really am going to listen to country records loud on the stereo and how I am going to find out whoever the hell I am. I'll be completely on my tod after all. Alone and able to get some real perspective on things. And seconds after luxuriating in that thought, I ask Steph Baber to come with me.

She says no. She smiles as she tells me that it seems a bit risky, a bit dramatic, like it might be skipping a few important stages. That it might end in tears.

'Besides,' she says. 'I haven't forgotten that you almost killed me. You remember that right? Lady in a yellow coat giving you the finger?'

A pause.

'Ah,' I say.

'Ah, indeed.' She is smiling though. Laughing as I squirm. My heart jumps again. 'Don't worry. I'm over it,' she says.

The air around us crackles and sparks. You can feel it. Almost see it.

I could have made a bit of a speech at this point, I guess. Could have said something about how every fully lived life should involve the risk of emotional damage. That it is a duty to take this risk, to love and feel without defence or reserve. Which is something I'd heard on the radio this this morning. But I don't.

'You think I'm insane,' I say.

'I think you might have impulse control issues at the very least. I'm flattered though. I think. How long are you going for?'

I shrug. Very devil-may-care.

'Well, I'll still be here. It's possible that I'll meet the man of my dreams while you're away but unlikely given that I have been on my own for ten years.'

'Would be just my luck.'

'Anyway, assuming that hasn't happened, let's meet for lunch or something when you're back.'

'Not lunch,' I say. 'Lunch is not for lovers.'

'Yes, you're right. Lovers don't do lunch.'

There is a pause, both of us smiling inanely. Then she excuses herself. 'I need to go and talk to Rosie and Ken,' she says.

Like a hardy weed fighting for the light, the possibility of new love pushes a way through the cracked concrete of my heart. I'm not mental though. I do know that maybe it won't be happy ever after with Steph. Maybe I'll never even see her again. Maybe Selena will actually call and ask me to rescue her from the staggering tedium of hiking through the Dolomites with Idiot Boy.

Anything could happen. It probably won't. But it might.

ACKNOWLEDGEMENTS

Thanks are due to: Arts Council England; Arvon Foundation; Mandy Appleyard; Tony and Janet Cropper; Sarah Crown; Robert Davidson; David Street Café, Holbeck; Eller café, Ossett; Dr Jim English; the keen-eyed and rigorous Kay Farrell; Sue Foot; Emma Forster; Moira Forsyth; David Gaffney; Grill and Griddle, Halifax; Ceris Jones; Alice Laing; Caron May; Herbie May; Mooch, Hebden Bridge; Carol Ockelford; Hannah Procter; Station Café, Hebden Bridge; Pete Stones; Towngate Tearooms, Heptonstall.

www.sandstonepress.com

 facebook.com/SandstonePress/

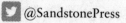 @SandstonePress